D0712839

DEATH OF A NEXT-DOOR NEIGHBOR

DEATH OF A NEXT-DOOR NEIGHBOR

David Goodnough

Walker and Company
New York

Copyright © 1988 by David Goodnough

All rights reserved. No part of this book may be reproduced or transmitted in any form or by any means, electronic or mechanical, including photocopying, recording, or by any information storage and retrieval system, without permission in writing from the Publisher.

All the characters and events portrayed in this story are fictitious.

First published in the United States of America in 1988 by the Walker Publishing Company, Inc.

Published simultaneously in Canada by Thomas Allen & Son Canada, Limited, Markham, Ontario.

Library of Congress Cataloging-in-Publication Data
Goodnough, David.
Death of a next-door neighbor / David Goodnough.
p. cm.
ISBN 0-8027-5703-0
I. Title.
PS3557.0586D4 1988 87-29044
813'.54--dc19 CIP

Printed in the United States of America
10 9 8 7 6 5 4 3 2 1

For Doris

His morning walk was beneath the elms in the church; 'for death,' he said, 'had been his next-door neighbour for so many years, that he had no apology for dropping the acquaintance.'

— Sir Walter Scott,
A Legend of Montrose

DEATH OF A NEXT-DOOR NEIGHBOR

1

HENRY WILNOT (PRONOUNCED will-nut) stepped from the back door of his house and into the bright summer sunshine. He faced the new day with confidence and a pleasurable anticipation, rather like an alcoholic with a bottle in the toolshed and plenty of work to do around the yard.

His feeling of well-being was dampened by the sound of a slamming door and the sight of his neighbor, Joe Casewait, making his way from his back porch toward the unsightly raised swimming pool to the rear of his property. Casewait was still clad in pajamas, bathrobe, and slippers, and appeared unsteady on his feet.

Loaded, thought Henry, and glanced disapprovingly at his watch. Seven twenty in the morning! He heard a car door *thunk* shut and an engine start. The car was hidden from his view as it roared off down the short bypass that ran from the main town road past the fronts of the two isolated houses, his and Casewait's.

This irritated Henry. He had heard the splattering of gravel onto the verge of his lawn as the car took off with spinning wheels—gravel that would eventually come into contact with the wounded blade of his ancient rotary lawn mower, delivering yet more blows that would finally kill it.

Henry was usually careful to check any vehicle that parked on the bypass, a favorite spot for libidinous teenagers by night and sleepy salesmen by day. Once or twice a month he policed the area of empty pints, beer cans, pizza crusts, and other traces of the affluent society that flourished nearby.

The bypass carved out a small island of land like an oxbow in front of his house and Casewait's, further separating them from the lightly traveled main road. On the far side of Henry's house, a meadowlike lawn ended at a haphazard stone wall that separated his property from a genuine forest. This belonged to a Catholic girls' college whose main buildings were situated more than half a mile away. On the side of the house where Henry stood, a blacktop driveway badly in need of sealing led to a detached garage farther to the rear. Beyond the driveway a narrow stretch of lawn sloped to a ragged border of fir trees and ill-kept shrubs that defined the property of his neighbor.

Where *was* Casewait, by the way? Henry had assumed that he was either heading for a morning swim to sober up, which was highly uncharacteristic of him—sobering up, not swimming—or pursuing some matter of imagined urgency such as adding chlorine to his precious pool or skimming its surface of airborne rubbish. Casewait perennially filled his pool weeks before anyone else in the area and just as regularly paid for it in needless labor.

Henry heard a splash from the pool and decided to make a break for his studio while Casewait was still submerged in his polluted waters. He hurried up the narrow walk that led past his garage to the small structure that stood at the fringe of the woods. Henry, a writer of original paperback novels—"original" in the sense that they had not previously appeared in hardcover—had long felt that he required a workplace separate from his home if he was to function at all. Early on he had found that he simply could not leave the breakfast table and go into another room and start typing. Accordingly, he had purchased the prefabricated shed he was rapidly approaching. He had seen it advertised in a heuristic gardening magazine that he read avidly, even though he couldn't seem to grow anything organically.

Actually, it was Casewait's daughter Jane who had a talent for growing things, and it was she who had taught Henry what little he did know about gardening. Jane, to his regret, had long since disappeared into one of the numerous self-discovery movements sweeping the land, leaving behind only a fond memory and the remnants of a patch of asparagus that resembled large weed, plus what seemed an endlessly renewing subscription to *Organic Gardening.*

The shed was apparently ideally intended to house a horse, which hadn't put Henry off too much; what the ad had failed to mention was that it didn't come with a floor. After taking one look at the easy-to-understand plans, Henry hired a carpenter (a harrowing experience, involving unprecedented expenditures) to construct a floor and raise the shed around it. Henry's son Harold, who was then going through a musical phase—he had formed and played lead guitar in a rock group and was of necessity a skilled electrician—had run a simple utility line from the house to the shed to serve his father's needs, which were furnished by one desk lamp and an electric heater, and Henry was soon in business and had been for some time now.

Carrying his thermos of coffee and a brown bag containing the lunch that his wife, a late sleeper, had prepared for him the night before, Henry plied his contented if slightly hurried way to the seat of his labors. Clad in washable poplin slacks and a light drip-dry shirt—indeed, his whole ensemble, including his ankle-high suede shoes, could be dipped in soapy water and hung up to dry, with Henry still in it if it came to that—he seemed to approximate the suburban ideal. In his early fifties, his thinning hair only slightly gray and minus the pompadour that he felt had trivialized his youth, his reasonably trim figure flawed only by a thickening about the waist, the result of literally thousands of ruinous lunches in the city, Henry had achieved that stage of life in which he was openly admired by supermarket cashiers and deferred to by minor public servants. He was moderately satisfied with most things in his life, with the exception of his children, of course, and he had the feeling that this personal contentment more than anything else was the cause of Casewait's estrangement.

For they had once been friends. The isolated situation of their houses—at the far side of Casewait's was a large empty tract that had never been developed—had naturally drawn them together. When Henry still worked in the city they had been fellow commuters to Manhattan and had taken turns driving to the station. They had even shared ownership of expensive gardening equipment, that ultimate in suburban male bonding. Added to this was the fact that their wives genuinely liked and got along with each other. But after Henry started working at home full time and to all appearances had prospered, the relationship between them had become strained.

Henry reached his studio and immediately sensed that something was out of the ordinary. Usually at this hour he would kick up a few rabbits or disturb the crows feeding upon his compost heap, but this morning the forest and its creatures were unnaturally silent. There also were none of the splashing sounds or seallike noises that Casewait usually made when disporting in his atrocious pool.

Henry unlocked the door to the shed and surveyed the interior for any signs of new inroads by the colony of squirrels he supported. The large writing table with chair and typewriter, the bookshelf with the basic writer's library and the bottle of vodka, which he used occasionally to unblock, and the armchair in which he mused over imaginary TV or picture deals were in their places on the disastrously expensive and now slightly uneven floor.

He put his thermos and lunch bag on the table and turned to close the door; something outside caught his eye. At the edge of his property there was a gap between a dying apple tree and a huge forsythia that allowed him a glimpse of Casewait's swimming pool, which jutted out of a downhill slope. Casewait was lying face down in the water, still in his pajamas and bathrobe, which was billowing out from his body.

Henry dashed across the lawn and through the gap in the

shrubbery and stumbled down the slope. He leapt onto the low wooden platform that circled the pool and was about to dive into the water, but he pulled up short of the edge. Surrounding Casewait's body and spreading beyond even the outspread bathrobe was a dark liquid that slowly streaked and then dissipated in the surrounding water. Henry knew what that was; he had been refining his description of it for years. It had oozed, spouted, clotted, run, dripped, and just plain bled from scores of his fictional characters. It was blood.

2

"AT FIRST I thought he'd hit his head," said Henry. He and the sheriff were standing on the platform of the pool.

"You aren't too wet," said the sheriff. "How'd you get him out?" Henry thought that the sheriff eyed him suspiciously.

"Over there," he said, motioning to a long pole with a net used for fishing leaves and other debris out of the water.

It was now eight thirty, but it seemed to Henry only moments ago that he had maneuvered Casewait to the edge with the pole and dragged him onto the platform. Up to that point he had been acting instinctively, but when he had turned the body over he had gone into mild shock, and the following few minutes were not too clear in his memory. For Henry, notwithstanding the frequency with which they turned up in his fiction, had never seen a corpse before, unless one counted aged relatives and dissolute acquaintances laid out in funeral homes. At first, upon viewing Casewait's face—the open, fixed eyes, the usually flushed face now pale, the mouth fixed in that rictus he had read so much about—Henry recoiled. But then he spent some time examining his onetime friend's body, possibly for the purpose of using him in a future case for Clagen, one of his more successful characters, who specialized in investigating crimes of violence.

The body had a large wound beneath the sternum that was still—no other word for it—oozing blood. Dark scabs of clotted blood surrounded the orifice and stained the bright paisley pajamas Casewait favored. The shot had obviously been fired at close range from a large-caliber gun ("A foreign job," Clagen would say, "probably a Schnauzer"—Henry was poor on guns and in the heat of creation called everything a

Schnauzer until he had a chance to look up a likely one in *The Encyclopedia of World Firearms,* one of his basic texts). How could it have happened? Henry had not heard a shot. Was it suicide? God knows Casewait had enough reasons for doing away with himself, but most people shoot themselves in the head, not the chest, and few would use a silencer even if they had one.

"What did you do after you dragged him up here?" asked the sheriff. It seemed a curious question to Henry, who could have thought of any number of different questions to ask about the situation, but he proceeded to tell him. . . .

Henry had done what he always did lately when confronted with something he didn't understand or couldn't control: he yelled for his wife, Erica. "Casewait has been shot!" he shouted as he bounded back across the lawn and onto the back porch of his house. "Call the police!" He heard some stirrings from upstairs but knew from experience that it would take Erica at least five minutes to achieve full consciousness. He went to the kitchen wall phone and dialed the police emergency number that was taped to the side of the phone. He waited for at least ten rings and then hung up and dialed the number of the police station listed in the phone book.

After five or six rings a bored voice answered. Henry, who had dealt with these people before, what with his troubles over the uses of the road in front of his house, said very slowly, "My name is Henry Wilnot"—he spelled out his name—"and I live at thirty-four Hardstone Road. My next-door neighbor, Joseph Casewait"—he spelled that name out also—"who lives at thirty-six Hardstone Road, has been shot in the chest and is dead."

"What?"

Henry repeated what he had said, even more carefully this time.

"Who is this?" asked the voice.

Henry repeated his name and address.

"All right, Mr. Wilnot," said the voice, "what's your problem?"

"My neighbor, Mr. Joseph Casewait, of thirty-six Hardstone Road has been shot and is dead. I just found him."

"Who was that again?"

Henry repeated the information gladly. This little colloquy was having a soothing effect on him, calming his nerves and returning him to rationality. The voice at the other end broke off and Henry was left to ponder the state of communication if not the whole complex relationship between citizen and civil servant.

At this point Erica felt her way into the kitchen. "Ach! Vot's heppenink?" As she got further into the morning, Henry knew, she would lose her accent, but just now it was barely eight o'clock and she was unable to cope with reality, let alone English.

"Casewait has been shot. I think he's dead," said Henry. "Sit down and have some coffee—or *make* some." He returned to the phone. "Yes," he said. "Well, you know where the town line crosses the college grounds?" he then gave the officer detailed instructions on how to find his house. These fellows had been known to get lost before.

Henry finally hung up and took the coffeepot from Erica's hands—she seemed to have dozed off while standing up—and put it on the counter next to the sink and plugged it in. He led Erica to the kitchen table and eased her into a chair and proceeded to explain to her what had happened.

"Oh, how horrible for Jeanette!" she said, finally realizing what had happened.

"Jeanette?" said Henry. "I thought she hated the—" He stopped himself. Naturally Erica would think of Jeanette, Casewait's estranged wife; she and Erica had been closest friends until Jeanette had decamped for California, where, according to Erica, she had found a new love and was preparing to shed herself completely of Casewait. It suddenly occurred to Henry that there was no one he could call on to take care of Casewait—or rather, his body. Casewait's parents were dead, and he had no brothers or sisters that Henry knew of. There was just Jeanette and Jane, Casewait's daughter by his first marriage, and they were both thousands of miles away.

"Maybe you'd better start thinking of calling Jeanette," said Henry. "No, wait, I'll do it, but try to get her address or telephone number or anything else that might help." He left her and wandered back across the lawn to the pool that he had always despised, considering it a blight upon the landscape, but which had now, or shortly would, become infamous, or at least newsworthy for a day or two. He could already see the photographs that would appear in the local paper: a general view of their houses; the ghastly pool, probably with a black Maltese cross marking the spot where the body had been found; and even Henry himself, foolishly pointing to the platform where he had beached the hapless Casewait. He began to long for his horse-stall studio and the innocently violent world of his private eyes, his cowboys, and his spies.

When the police finally arrived they had advanced upon Henry, who was standing by the body, the way that infantry are taught to approach a fortified position. Crime was on the increase everywhere, and the local constabulary was as nervous as any patrolman assigned to one of the benighted areas of a great city. After Henry indicated by sign language—lifting his arms away from his body as if inviting a search—that he was unarmed, the officer in charge approached and sized up the situation by looking closely at Henry from head to toe. Then, true to the universal rule of law-enforcement agencies that the person who reports a crime is the most likely one to have committed it, he subjected Henry to a rigorous examination—name, address, occupation, and so forth.

Henry answered his questions with patience and equanimity. Such was his normal American opinion of the forces of the law that he was convinced that if he expressed any irritation or was openly critical of the way the investigation was conducted, he would be set upon and beaten about the head and shoulders with truncheons.

"Who's he?" asked the officer, finally taking notice of Casewait's body.

Henry told him, and filled in all the information about Casewait he had just supplied on himself. "Anybody in the house?" asked the officer.

My god! thought Henry. He hadn't even considered that. Of course someone must be in the house, or had been in the house. The sound of the car roaring off the road crossed his mind. "I don't know. He's been living alone," said Henry.

"Harley, you and Bierson search the house," said the officer to two young patrolmen who were staring with fascination at Casewait's corpse.

"What?" said Harley, who from the look on his face might have added, "Are you *crazy*?" He recovered quickly, however, and motioned to Bierson to follow him. Again Henry was reminded of the military. Harley flattened himself against the wall beside the back door, gun drawn, while Bierson kicked the door open. Harley rushed in, followed by Bierson.

The homeowner in Henry was repelled. "Was that necessary?" he asked the officer beside him. "I mean, don't you need a court order or a warrant or something?"

"A *warrant*," said the officer with as much scorn as he could muster. "Where the hell do you think you are? England?"

There didn't seem much for Henry to say to that, except that in fact he wished he were in England right now, so he kept his silence.

To judge by the sounds coming from Casewait's house, Harley and Bierson were conducting a room-by-room search similar to the mopping-up tactics used by the Russian Army upon entering Berlin. Henry was about to lodge a modest protest when two more police cars pulled up in front of Casewait's house, and with a great slamming of doors, four men emerged and walked around the side of the house to the rear. Since two of them were in plain clothes, Henry assumed they were detectives. He breathed a sigh of relief. Perhaps they could curb Harley and Bierson and start doing what was supposed to be done in these cases, such as cordoning off the area and searching for sign, Deerslayer fashion.

The police sergeant—for sergeant he was, as Henry had surmised by observing the stripes on sleeve—came alive at the sight of the new arrivals and hastened to meet them, leaving Henry standing rather self-consciously by the body. Was he then to be Casewait's only friend and companion, even in death as in life?

The sergeant had attached himself to the tallest man in the approaching group and guided him to the pool. "It's right over here, Sam," said the sergeant. "Watch your step, now." Deferential, thought Henry, to the well-known point of obsequiousness.

The tall man gained the platform and scrutinized his surroundings with a gaze Henry recognized as that he often ascribed to more than one of his fictional characters: sleepy-eyed, yet steady. The man's eyes came to rest upon Henry.

"This is the guy that found him," piped up the sergeant, who was acting more and more like a puppy dog yipping at the legs of its master. "He lives next door, name of "—he consulted his notebook—"Wilnot, Henry Wilnot."

"Will-nut," said Henry.

"Good morning," said the tall man, "I'm Sam Watnell. I understand you've had some trouble here."

The sheriff obviously intended to put Henry at his ease, but Henry wasn't buying it, for he had recognized the man as none other than Big Sam Watnell himself, perpetual candidate for county sheriff, who was ritually returned to office every three years by an electorate that existed, so far as Henry could tell, on the planet Mars. Watnell's ruthlessness and self-interest were legendary, and his talent for getting reelected was as uncanny as it was mysterious, since no one in the entire county had ever been known to say or hear a kind word about him. It went without saying that he was feared and respected, and Henry put himself on guard.

Henry had already told the sheriff everything he had previously related to the sergeant and was about to embark on new ground when Harley and Bierson emerged from the house, obviously relieved to be outside again. Harley shook his head at the sergeant, who turned to the sheriff and said, "Just checking the house out, Sam. Okay?" Big Sam was noncommittal, and the sergeant seemed to lose some of his confidence.

The sheriff glanced at Harley and Bierson, his face showing an expression of boredom and slight disdain. "Did these two know enough not to touch anything?" he asked.

Henry felt that he could have told him a thing or two about that, but he decided to keep his own counsel. The sergeant glared at Harley and Bierson, who were admitting nothing.

The sheriff motioned to his own contingent to follow him and headed toward the house. "The medical examiner's on his way," he said to the sergeant over his shoulder. "You know what to do?"

"Sure, Sam, sure," said the sergeant. "I'll take care of everything." Which, thought Henry, would consist of pointing out the body to the doctor.

"You might as well come with us," said the sheriff to Henry. "You know the house, don't you?"

"Used to," said Henry, falling in with the little group. "Haven't been inside for months though. We haven't been—I mean, we don't—*didn't* get along too well." Henry felt that he had just made himself the prime suspect in the sheriff's eyes.

"Argue, fight, what?" asked the sheriff.

"Well, you might say that we disagreed over my—or, that he was my severest critic." Henry thought that perhaps he should get himself a lawyer right away.

The sheriff looked at him sharply and was about to speak when the yelping, howling, barking and baying of what sounded like an enormous band of enraged dogs interrupted him. "What the hell is that?" he said.

"Just the Hardstone Kennels," said Henry. "The dogs are usually fed about this time."

"But that's not near here, is it?"

"No, it's about a mile away, but some sort of acoustical freakishness makes it seem like it's right next door."

"Oh," said the sheriff. "The Hardstone. That's where Desplaines keeps his itty-bitty dogs, isn't it?"

He was referring to Chief Thompson Desplaines, the township's socialite chief of police, who owned a pair of toy poodles that were his constant companions when he was in residence at his estatelike home.

"I imagine he does," said Henry, "when he's traveling. It's supposed to be very good."

"I'll bet it is," said the sheriff, revealing either contempt for or envy of Chief Desplaines. Probably a bit of both, thought Henry.

It occurred to Henry that the chief had jurisdiction in this part of the county, and that he or one of his men should be on the scene and conducting the investigation. True, the town police had been first on the scene, but they, or at least their sergeant, clearly seemed to be enthralled by the sheriff and prepared to do his bidding. Interesting, thought Henry, as he stepped up onto Casewait's back porch.

One of the uniformed patrolmen held the door open for them and they entered a small, tidy room inelegantly called a "mud room" by real estate agents, and passed through it into the kitchen. Henry was immediately struck by one thing: the kitchen was spotless, indeed gleaming. He had had visions of a sink piled with dirty dishes, trash cans overflowing with liquor and beer bottles, ashtrays filled with cigarette butts; but here everything was in order. An experienced hand had been over the place, and not too long ago either. There was not so much as a used glass on the drainboard. Not even Harley and Bierson had been able to disturb anything when they had stormed the house.

The sheriff and his group passed through the kitchen into the dining room. Same thing. The polished table and sideboard gleamed. A glance into the living room revealed the startling emptiness of a perfectly tidy house. The whole place seemed to cry out for a newspaper dropped beside an easy chair, an empty glass or some discarded knitting. Not even Jeanette, who had had a cleaning woman come in once a week, could have maintained this standard.

One thing was certain to Henry, however: Casewait could not have had anything to do with it. The man was—had been—a born slob, and bone lazy.

"Quite a place," said the sheriff, passing his finger over a dustless end table. "Did this guy have a maid or a cleaning lady?"

"Not that I know of," said Henry. "His wife left him about six months ago, and as far as I know he lived completely alone—when he was home at all, that is."

The sheriff raised an eyebrow. "He was away a lot?"

Henry filled him in on Casewait's recent history. An advertising executive who had flourished during the industry's golden age of the fifties and early sixties, Casewait had finally done what all advertising men yearn to do: he quit his job and opened his own shop. Perhaps he had been spurred on by the fact that he was losing most of his lucrative accounts and was about to lose his job anyway, but nevertheless he opened his new offices with a great deal of fanfare and a tremendous amount of ill will, resulting from his postemployment gossiping and spreading of tales about his former employers and clients. The creative people who had followed him into his new shop swiftly abandoned what they perceived to be a sinking ship, and those clients he had managed to maintain soon followed. Casewait was reduced to answering his own phone calls, preparing his own presentations, and legging it about the city in pursuit of clients, some of whose business was of such a dubious nature that his former colleagues would not touch them with a barge pole. This was not surprising to Henry, who had long heard rumors that Casewait was not always circumspect in his dealings.

"He still has—*had* an office in the city," continued Henry. "But I gathered that he spent a lot of time on the road or somewhere. I mean, the house was often dark on weekends, and sometimes even in the middle of the week. Of course, maybe he was merely working late and spent the night in the city— Look here, shouldn't someone be taking notes or something? Will I have to repeat all this later on?"

The sheriff's lack of interest in Henry's narrative was obvious. He was wandering around examining furniture and paintings more like an appraiser than a detective. "The locals will be taking your statement," he said somewhat distractedly, examining a porcelain bowl, which, thought Henry, probably shouldn't be handled at all at this stage of the investigation—if one could call it that.

"The locals?" said Henry. "Aren't you in charge of the investigation?"

"No-o," chuckled the sheriff. "That'll be for the town boys. They'll be along shortly and attend to all the details." He then proceeded serenely upstairs, apparently to examine whatever else took his fancy. Meanwhile the plainclothesman and the uniformed officer were nosing about in cupboards and closets with no discernible system or objective.

Henry felt that he should assert his rights somehow—although just what they were he was unsure. He would have to get in touch with his lawyer immediately, he told himself, troubled only slightly by the fact that he did not *have* a lawyer that he knew of. He followed the sheriff meekly upstairs.

"Did this guy usually make his own bed?" asked the sheriff from the master bedroom.

"As far as I know," said Henry, "Joe Casewait never made a bed in his life, except maybe in the army." And if there had been a way to get out of making your bed in the army, he was sure, Casewait would have found it.

Henry entered the bedroom and saw what Big Sam was getting at. The large double bed was wrinkle free and looked suspiciously as though under the covering bedspread and quilt it had been made up with hospital corners. Casewait had been wearing pajamas and bathrobe when he had been shot. Even if by some miracle he had made his own bed, it's likely that he would have waited until he was dressed, or about to get dressed.

The sheriff made no comment and continued his ruminative investigation. "Tell me, Mister . . . ?" he said.

"Wilnot," said Henry.

"Do you notice that anything is obviously missing?"

That's it? thought Henry, who had been expecting something revelatory, such as "Hello, what have we here?" or "What do you make of this, Wilnot?"

"No, not that I can tell just now," said Henry. Of course, he had not been in the house since Jeanette had left. That had been the day after a disastrous party at which Casewait had alienated not only Henry but just about everyone else within earshot. This had included a local music teacher who composed "portraits" of her acquaintances, a Sunday painter who had just had a show at a county gallery, and a poetess who contributed verse to the local giveaway newspaper. It was as if Casewait had purposely invited all of these artists manqués, Henry included, so that he could excoriate them for their pretensions. Which is exactly what he had done, in his cups and at length. He was particularly hard on a local writer of travel books who had scored a mild success with his latest one on Central Asia called *Loved*

Samarkand, Hated Ind. The title had made Casewait livid—probably because he hadn't thought of it himself, in Henry's opinion—and he and the writer had nearly come to blows. The writer, a burly fellow who carried a gnarled walking stick in keeping with his profession, looked as though he could dispatch Casewait with ease, and Henry had intervened between the two, thus gaining the ill will of both.

If it had been Casewait's wish to cut himself off completely from local society, he succeeded brilliantly. People fled the house, never to return, not even to collect for the United Fund. Casewait would have trouble drawing even Jehovah's Witnesses, who occasionally roamed the landscape in search of converts. After a terrific row, which Henry could not help overhearing from across the way, Jeanette had packed and left the next day for Los Angeles. Before her marriage to Casewait she had worked very successfully at a large talent agency, which later moved out there, and she was regularly offered her old job back. She decided to take it, and the last Henry had heard—through Erica, who maintained a waning correspondence with Jeanette—she was happily placing dogs and cats, as well as humans, in lucrative television commercials.

"Everything looks just about the same," said Henry, "only cleaner and neater, of course."

"Did this guy have any kids?" asked the sheriff, either changing the subject or, like most people, equating a house's neatness and order with the absence of children.

"One daughter, Jane," said Henry, "who's in Switzerland. Or was, the last time I heard. She attends a TM school—that's transcendental meditation; you know, the Maharishi or whatever he calls himself. She works for them, the TM people, or teaches, or both. I could never figure it out."

The sheriff couldn't have cared less, and he stood staring meditatively into space. Henry half expected to be treated to a deduction, but the sheriff's mood was broken when the plainclothesman stuck his head into the room and muttered, "Morris is here, Sam."

"Yeah, I suppose he is," said the sheriff, who didn't seem at all pleased. He strode out of the bedroom and down the stairs. Henry, confused, stared after him, and said to the plainclothesman, "Doesn't he need me anymore?"

"I guess not," said the officer, following the sheriff. "The local will want to see you, though. You might as well go home and wait."

"You mean I can just leave?" said Henry, who had almost expected to spend the rest of the day seated at a bare table at police headquarters surrounded by hard cases in their shirt sleeves and wearing shoulder holsters.

"Sure. You just live next door. And you aren't going anywhere," he added. Needlessly, thought Henry.

"Who's Morris?" he asked as he tagged after the officer, who was following the sheriff.

"The local," he said with what sounded to Henry like contempt.

As he crossed the lawn toward his house, Henry saw that a new car had arrived and two men were approaching the house by the front walk. The sheriff was advancing to meet them, followed by his trusty lieutenant, the plainclothesman. The sergeant in charge of the uniformed officers seemed to have made himself scarce and could be seen snooping around on the far side of the pool, as far away as he could get from the front of the house.

3

HENRY INDEED WAS not going anywhere; within another hour the parked police cars and the ropes and barriers that cordoned off the small road in front of the two houses had effectively isolated the enclave. Photographers had come, along with the medical examiner and an ambulance to remove the body when the ME was through with it. Henry repeated his statement to the young police officer and stenographer who showed up at his front door and then waited patiently for the next development in this extraordinary day.

It was now nearly one o'clock and Henry, when not peeking out of his side windows at the proceedings next door, had had time only to make a phone call to a lawyer named Thomas Scanlon, whom he had met while spending time on jury duty the year before. The young fellow had been handling a case to which Henry had been assigned, and he had questioned Henry closely before dismissing him for cause; however, he had seemed genuinely interested in Henry and what he had to say. Henry had sought him out afterward, hoping to pump him for some information on trial procedure that he thought he might be able to use in one of McMurdoo's capers. McMurdoo was another one of Henry's private eyes, but of a more conservative bent, who actually had to testify in court now and then. Scanlon had seemed flattered and pleased, and cooperated to the extent of sending Henry a letter containing some additional information he thought might be useful to him.

Henry was somewhat surprised to reach Scanlon on his first try. He had heard that the young lawyer was now one of the busiest in the county, due to a fresh outbreak of civil rights cases—not the old-fashioned kind involving school busing and job discrimination, but the new variety, which invoked the basic human right to break the law. Shortly after Henry had met him, Scanlon had gotten the scion of one of the county's wealthiest and most socially prominent families declared innocent of a drugs-possession charge, and he had become the instant hero of the local youth culture. "Get Scanlon," became the cry of college students thrown in the slammer for burning down the science building. "I want to see Scanlon," became the demand of the rock musician the contents of whose car could render a good-size community comatose. Scanlon was obviously a man on the way up.

The man was also clearly harassed. "Christ!" said Scanlon after reassuring Henry that he remembered him. "I've got a case in the city where these two illegal aliens applied for unemployment insurance and when they didn't get it tried to set fire to the unemployment office. I'm on my way there now. What's the world coming to?" he asked cheerfully. "So what can I do for you?"

Henry explained what had happened and asked for general advice. He didn't insult the lawyer by indicating that he would pay for any information forthcoming, since he knew perfectly well that Scanlon had punched one of those clocks that tournament chess players use and was contentedly watching the dollars tick away.

"Just tell the truth," said Scanlon, "and don't leave anything out, provided that it's not self-incriminating. They couldn't get you even on that, but just don't give them any unnecessary ideas. And watch out for Big Sam; he's murder." The man was off and running after a hurried "If they give you any trouble, get in touch with me or my office. Someone will be here to help if I'm not."

Sound enough advice, thought Henry as he hung up the phone—probably about the same as he could have gotten from the produce man at the supermarket—but Scanlon's cheerfulness and lack of concern was infectious, and Henry felt slightly better for the conversation. But why watch out for Big Sam?

Henry had made the call from the phone extension in his bedroom. He went back down to the kitchen and joined his wife for lunch—or, rather, another cup of coffee. His prepared lunch was still in his work shed, but he didn't feel up to getting it. He glanced fondly at his wife, who was now dressed and who fully comprehended what had happened.

Erica was the only lazy German Henry had ever met, and he found the contrast with the national image appealing. He would probably have felt the same toward a diffident Frenchman or a taciturn Italian. Henry had met her in Stuttgart, where he had spent a rather pleasant tour of duty during the height of the Korean War. He had seen her first at a concert when his attention had wandered and he had spotted a striking blonde sitting in the row just behind him. He saw her again at a performance of the Stuttgart Ballet (the *old* Stuttgart Ballet, which those who saw it are still trying to forget). Henry, who had majored in estheticism in college, was naturally drawn to these events, and she may have noticed him at one or another; in any event, she seemed to recognize him, and he nodded to her and smiled; she had smiled back. That did it as far as Henry was concerned.

In both encounters she had been escorted by a Viking who wore one of those postwar German suits that was cut like the Tin Man's outfit in *The Wizard of Oz*. Henry himself was all soft flannel, with button-down shirt and knit tie, which, combined with the insouciance that only an off-duty company clerk could command, must have proved irresistible. Anyway, the next time he saw her she actually spoke to him, which was remarkable in the fact that most well-brought-up German girls would not have anything to do with an American soldier.

It was at one of the brave little social-musical events that the Seventh Army was forever staging to convince the locals that not every American was a clotted-bummed yahoo. This was a losing battle all the way, of course, but it did give soldiers like Henry a chance to meet German girls outside of Blowhole Alley, the name the GIs had given to Stuttgart's red-light district. She was alone (the Viking turned out to be a cousin), and Henry struck up a conversation with her in his gasthaus German, but they soon switched to English after he invited her to have coffee in the PX at the service club. They began seeing each other, even though Erica's father objected strongly. He was connected with Mercedes-Benz and was well on his way to making his first million, and the last thing in the world he wanted was for his only daughter to be knocked up by some Yank. But for Henry it was a proper relationship, and he continued to correspond with her after he rotated to the States and was discharged.

Erica talked her father into letting her take part in a student exchange program, and she and Henry found each other again. After a discreet period they announced their engagement, and Erica's father demanded that she return to Germany immediately. Henry told him to go to hell, effectively canceling thereby his plans to continue graduate school and lead the pleasant academic life he had planned for himself. He took a job in the then burgeoning publishing industry, and he and Erica had married immediately. Now, nearly thirty years later, Henry had few regrets—except his children, of course—and for his wife a tender regard.

The phone on the wall behind Erica rang, and she reached behind her back, lifted the receiver, brought it forward over her head and tucked it under her chin in one flowing movement, like a tennis service that has been perfected after long practice and devotion to the game. "Hello," she said, and after a few seconds her face crumpled, she sniffed, and tears sprang to her eyes. "Oh, Jeanette," she wailed, "I'm so *sorry*." A long pause followed. "This morning. Henry found him. . . .You'd better talk to him; he's right here." She handed the receiver to Henry, whispering, "Jeanette."

"I know," said Henry, taking the receiver. "Hello, Jeanette."

"Henry, what happened?" said the no-nonsense voice at the other end. "Some idiot called and said Joe's been shot." Henry had always liked Jeanette, even if she was pretty much the show business type he mildly disapproved of—mostly because they all seemed to find his work unplayable.

"I'm sorry, Jeanette, I would have called you myself but the police said they'd handle it." It had seemed to Henry that they had implied they knew better how to handle these delicate situations. He wondered whether they had assigned Bierson or Harley to the task. He went on to tell Jeanette what had happened. By now he had told his story at least four times and he had polished it in the intervals between recitations so he was able to give her the whole picture in no more than a minute. "So I got him out of the pool and called the police," he ended.

"What the hell was he doing in that goddamn pool?" she nearly shouted. Jeanette shared Henry's feelings about Casewait's pool.

"Don't ask me," said Henry. "The police act as though I put him there. In fact, right now I think I'm the prime suspect. Heh-heh." He wondered if he should get someone to recommend a lawyer besides Scanlon.

"Oh, for God's sake!" said Jeanette, with disgust. "Look, I'm on my way to the airport. I don't know when I'll be able to get a flight, so don't you or Erica try to meet me. I'll take a cab or rent a limousine or something."

"Is there anything we can do in the meantime?" he asked. "Can we notify Jane for you? I wouldn't want to trust the police to do that."

"Oh, God, I hate to do it myself, but I'll have to when I get there," she said. "To tell the truth, I'm not even sure where she is. Thanks anyway. Listen, I've got to run. Sorry I can't talk to Erica, but we'll have a real gab fest when I get settled in. See you."

"See you," said Henry, and hung up. Not one word of regret or sorrow, he thought. Well, who could blame her?

"Here comes another detective," said Erica, who had left her chair while Henry was on the phone and was now looking out of the kitchen window.

"It's the one who took over from the sheriff this morning," said Henry, looking over Erica's shoulder at the slender middle-aged man coming up the driveway.

Detective Lieutenant Morris introduced himself in the traditional manner, flipping his wallet open to his ID. In true suburban fashion, he had come to the back door instead of the front, and he entered the kitchen at Henry's invitation. After he was installed in a chair at the breakfast table and supplied with a cup of coffee, he got down to business.

"Mr. Wilnot," he began, "we have your statement, of course, but there are some tangential matters that we'd like to take up with you." Henry immediately distrusted the man. Anyone who would use the word *tangential* as part of ordinary discourse was capable of anything, as far as he was concerned. Of all the words in the English language, Henry considered it one of the most infelicitous, fit only for the palaver of sports commentators and lawyers.

"Now," said the lieutenant, "you've told us of Mr. Casewait's business affairs, but I wonder if you could elaborate on them. Did you ever visit his office, for instance?"

"No," said Henry. "By the time he had established his own business we were scarcely on speaking terms."

"What was the nature of your argument, if I might ask?"

"We disagreed on artistic matters," said Henry, rather loftily. "He didn't care for my work and I didn't consider his worthy of noticing, let alone discussing."

"I see," said the lieutenant, though Henry couldn't understand how he possibly could. His skepticism must have showed, for the officer went on, "We have run into quite a few disputes like this—I mean the type you are describing—which is understandable, given the socioeconomic and intellectual makeup of the population in this area."

What the hell have we got here? thought Henry. Since when have they taught pop sociology at the police academy?

"What I'm trying to find out, Mr. Wilnot, is whether Mr. Casewait was in financial straits. Did he have any money troubles that you were aware of?"

"I really can't say. I never knew anything about his financial affairs. I just assumed that he had enough to live comfortably. There were never any bill collectors knocking at his door that I know of, and I've never been questioned about him by any collection agencies or anything. He always seemed to live up to a certain standard: theater tickets, dinners, parties—if he could find anyone who would attend them—country club, vacations. That sort of thing."

"I see," said the lieutenant, making a mark in his notebook. "Now, then," he said looking up at Henry, who was on his feet, pacing back and forth. "Do you know if Mr. Casewait ever had any contact with what for want of a better term we might call a criminal element?"

My God, thought Henry, are they teaching arch dialogue too at the police academy these days? "You mean the mob, the syndicate, the . . . Mafia?" he said, falling into Lieutenant Morris's speech pattern. "No, not that I know of, although he kept some pretty racy company in the city. I mean, in advertising, publishing, any phase of the entertainment business, there're always things like kickbacks, favors, money on the side; but nothing really *organized*. I really don't know if Casewait was that important, if he was in a position to warrant anyone to . . . what? Tempt him?"

"I see," said the lieutenant, snapping his notebook closed. "Thank you very much, you've been most helpful. And now I'll just be on my way."

"Do you mind if I ask," said Henry, "why you suspect that Casewait was connected with a criminal element?"

"We don't suspect it, Mr. Wilnot. We are just trying to

find out if there *was* a connection."

Hmm, thought Henry. There must be a distinction there somewhere. He would have to mull it over later. "I'll bet I know what it is," he said.

"Oh?" said the lieutenant.

"Casewait was shot with a large-caliber gun, right? And I never heard a shot. That would imply a silencer, wouldn't it?"

"Yes," said the lieutenant; he seemed amused. "And your point?"

"Well, your average murderer, or even anyone intent on mischief, would have trouble laying his hands on a silencer. I mean, they don't sell them at your local sporting goods store, do they?"

"Indeed they do not, Mr. Wilnot; in fact, silencers are against the law. Perhaps you have a point. Well, I must run. Thanks again for your time."

Henry accompanied him to the door. Before leaving, the lieutenant said somewhat diffidently, "By the way, Mr. Wilnot, I don't suppose you have any inkling as to why or how Mr. Casewait was killed."

"No," said Henry. "I'm as completely in the dark as you are." A nice touch, that, he thought. "All I know is that he got himself shot somehow and then drowned in his wretched pool."

"Quite," said Detective Lieutenant Morris, and took his departure.

"Damn!" said Henry, as he watched the detective walk down the drive. He expected his policemen to be plodding and relentless, not arch and brittle. And what was all this business about organized crime?

4

JEANETTE ARRIVED AFTER midnight via rented car from the airport, wearing the martyred expression of Californians who have put up with twenty or thirty miles of the merely four-lane highways of the northeast. She and Erica fell into each other's arms and retired to the kitchen for the inevitable coffee.

"I came right here," said Jeanette. "You don't mind do you? I just couldn't face that house."

"Of course not," said Erica. "You'll stay here; I've got Gretchen's room all ready for you."

"Henry," said Jeanette, "what do I have to do? I haven't the slightest idea how to behave in these cases. Do I have to see Joe, identify him or anything like that? Oh, God, I just can't get used to it. I made it pretty clear how I felt about him, but . . . "

"We understand," said Henry. And so will the rest of the county when they hear about it, he might have added. "I've already identified him and given the police the basic information. I imagine your biggest problem will be winding up his affairs"—he winced at the word; Casewait had been a notorious womanizer—"but you can probably get a lawyer or a bank officer to do most of it."

"You'll help me, won't you Henry?" she said pleadingly.

Henry had always found her attractive, and she could still get a flush from him. She had been Casewait's second wife. His first wife had died shortly after Casewait had moved out from the city with her and his daughter, so Henry had not known her well. Casewait had then married Jeanette, who had worked at a modeling agency his firm did business with, and he had lost little time in installing her in his home as enforced laborer and nanny-companion for his daughter Jane.

"Of course I will," said Henry. "How about Jane, though? Do you still want to get in touch with her yourself? By the way, where is she? Gretchen says she looked her up in Lausanne, but that was about three months ago." Gretchen was Henry's second child, the light of his life for her first sixteen years and the bane of his existence thereafter—along with his son, of course. She had been backpacking in Europe for almost six months now, and Henry regularly tortured himself with seduction-of-innocents scenes remembered from old European movies, scenes involving sinister inns and evil-looking haystacks.

"I heard from her just last week," said Jeanette. "One of those dreadful blue aerograms or whatever they call them that you can't open without destroying. She should be in Paris now, taking part in some sort of symposium; probably working like a dog for the delegates or whatever they call themselves. You know, all they do is sit around and meditate while poor slaves like Jane cook and wash up and generally kill themselves for them. It's a good thing she's got a cleaning compulsion." Jeanette had spent some time in analysis, so any character trait or mere tendency in others was easily explained away as a compulsion.

"I've got the number of her hotel here somewhere," she said, rummaging in her bag, which looked like a soft leather version of the sort of sack Henry had used delivering papers as a boy. "Here it is," she said, extracting a crumpled piece of blue paper. "The Hotel du Plessis. What time is it over there? It must be nearly seven o'clock. I wonder if she's up. God, one never knows what these kids are up to nowadays."

Jane was twenty-six if she was a day, thought Henry, and could hardly be classified as a kid, and yet she was allied with these maharishis—how many were there, anyway?—and somehow one placed the age of their followers at around sixteen, be they rock stars or aging movie actresses. "It's just about a quarter to seven there now," he said. "Why not give her an hour or so? But she's probably been up for hours if she has to cater to those yogis." Was that right? Were maharishis yogis? "I think I'd better call the police and tell them that you're here. The chief or the sheriff or a detective lieutenant will probably want to take a statement from you. Remember now, these people are devoted to paperwork, so try to indulge them. I've given my statement at least four times."

Henry dialed the familiar number and after the usual delay finally got through. He asked for Detective Lieutenant Morris and was surprised to find that he was in. What were these quintessential suburbanites, the police, doing up at this hour? "Hello, Lieutenant," he said, "good to talk to you again."

"My pleasure," said the lieutenant.

Henry informed him that Jeanette had arrived and would be available for grilling in the morning. "Excellent," said the lieutenant. "I'll try to be there around ten o'clock, and I'll bring the key to her house, if she doesn't have one." Henry said that was fine and was just about to hang up when the lieutenant added, "By the way, we found a copy of Mr. Casewait's will. It's not the original, of course, but it's simple enough and will probably match the one in his lawyer's office or wherever he kept it. I don't think I'm breaking any rules in telling you that you were named coexecutor of his estate, along with Mrs. Casewait."

"What!" said Henry. What was this all about? And since when didn't cops know all the rules? Then he remembered that some time ago, when they were more than tolerable friends, Casewait had mentioned something about their making each other executors of their respective estates. That must have been ten years ago, and it had surprised Henry at the time that Casewait was prudent enough to concern himself with matters such as wills and estates, and he had promptly dismissed it from his mind.

"Don't worry," said the lieutenant, "it's a fairly conventional will. No surprises; everything goes to the wife and daughter. There's also a letter to you from the deceased. It was folded inside the will. I'll bring it—that is, a copy of it—along tomorrow." The lieutenant hung up, leaving a slightly mystified Henry staring at the receiver.

"What's wrong, dear?" said Erica. She and Jeanette had returned from the upstairs, where the guest had been installed in Gretchen's old room.

"Nothing. The detective lieutenant will be here tomorrow at about ten. Do you have an alibi, Jeanette?"

"It's a good thing I was three thousand miles away," said Jeanette, "otherwise I'd be the prime suspect, don't you think?"

"I'm sorry, Jeanette," said Henry, "I was just joking." This depressed Henry, since it reminded him that *he* was probably the prime suspect. "Why don't I try to get through to Jane now?" he said, mostly to change the subject. "Maybe the maharishis have an early meditation hour. Do you have the number?"

"Here," said Jeanette, about to pass to him the crumpled aerogram. "No, I'd better copy it out for you. It's complicated." She took a pen from her voluminous handbag and copied out the number on a paper napkin. "I don't know much about Paris, but it doesn't sound like a particularly good address."

Probably some notorious fleabag, thought Henry, catering to students and North African terrorists. He thought of his own daughter in these surroundings and shuddered. He dialed the overseas operator and gave her the number. While waiting, it occurred to him that he could not speak French. Read it, sing it, yes; but speak it? Forget it! "Here, Erica, you'd better handle this," he said to his wife, handing her the receiver. He had absolute faith in the linguistic virtuosity of Germans, though he could not recall ever hearing Erica speak a word of any language other than German or English.

When the connection was finally made, Erica conducted the whole conversation in English, which the party at the other end apparently had little trouble in understanding and speaking. "She's not there," said Erica. "They have held her room for her, but she hasn't shown up yet. What shall I tell them?"

"That's odd," said Jeanette. "She was supposed to have been there yesterday. Or was it today? God, I can't tell what day it is or what time it is with all this traveling all over the place. Why don't you just tell them to have her call us as soon as she arrives? She can reverse the charges or whatever they do over there. I'm really not up to all of this," she said as an afterthought, and Henry had a foreboding that she was not going to be much help as his coexecutor of the Casewait estate. The troubles surrounding a reclusive millionaire's will had only recently been in the news, and Henry had a brief premonition of a court case in which his competency might be brought into question.

Erica concluded her conversation with the clerk at the distant hotel by repeating her phone number two or three times and hanging up with an "*auf wiedersehen.*" So much for linguistic virtuosity.

"Look," said Henry, "we'd better all turn in. You must be exhausted, Jeanette, and Erica's getting silly. I'll just clear things up." They departed gratefully for their rooms while Henry rinsed cups and glasses and deposited them in the dishwasher. He then poured himself a stiff Scotch and sat down at the kitchen table to ponder his predicament. It was not in the least pleasant. Not only to his mind was he a prime suspect in a murder, but he was also saddled with the sort of responsibility he disliked intensely, since he knew full well that he would have to see it through to the end. But there was one other matter that was beginning to impinge itself on his consciousness, something that not even the police had so far mentioned. There was a gunman loose somewhere.

5

THE FOLLOWING MORNING Henry hovered about the front rooms of his house, peering through the blinds like some lethal housekeeper in a Hitchcock film. When he spied Detective Lieutenant Morris coming up the drive, he nipped into his study, a small room to the rear of the house, which he used when the temperature dropped below freezing and rendered his horse barn untenable. He settled into an easy chair, popped a cold pipe into his mouth, opened a random volume, and awaited the sound of the great thundering boots of the constable.

Actually, Detective Lieutenant Morris was wearing shoes of Italian workmanship so supple that he seemed to be walking in his stocking feet. He tapped lightly on the back door and was admitted by Erica, who had arisen early in deference to her houseguest, Jeanette.

"Is your husband here, Mrs. Wilnot?" asked the lieutenant. "I'd like to speak to him for a moment, if I may."

"Yes, of course," said Erica. "I'll fetch him straightaway." The lieutenant seemed to have set a conversational pattern that even Erica, who had proven herself linguistically insensitive, was caught up in. With the aplomb of a character in a boulevard drama, she left the room and summoned her spouse.

"Ah, there, Detective Lieutenant," said Henry as he entered the room.

"Mr. Wilnot," said the lieutenant, nodding in greeting and keeping the conversational ball rolling. "I'm sorry to have to bother you again, but there are a few details we would like to know a little more about." After seating himself, he consulted his ever handy notebook. "You said in your statement that the deceased, Mr. Casewait, came out of his house at exactly seven twenty and walked or staggered toward his swimming pool, where you found him floating about two or three minutes later. Could you determine that he was actually headed for his swimming pool rather than somewhere else on his property?"

"You mean that you think he was trying to get somewhere besides the pool? I doubt it. Unless he was looking for something out in that field of weeds he called a lawn."

The flicker of interest that passed over the detective's face told Henry that he had hit upon something. "Are you familiar with his lawn, Mr. Wilnot?" asked Morris.

"I used to be," said Henry, "when we shared gardening chores." Actually, Henry knew the lawn well. It was in even worse shape than his own.

"Do you happen to know of any convenient hiding place, perhaps a hole of some sort, that might be used as a cache for, say, a briefcase or a fairly large box?"

"I see what you're getting at," said Henry. "You think Casewait was trying to retrieve something after he was shot. Have you tried the pool itself? That seems to me the most obvious place, since he was headed toward it and eventually drowned in it."

"We're draining the pool later today," said the detective lieutenant, "but our preliminary search indicates we'll be lucky to find anything new."

Anything new? thought Henry. What had they already found? The detective lieutenant, perhaps reading his thoughts, gave him an owlish look and true to police procedure did not elaborate on his remark.

"Now I wonder if I might see Mrs. Casewait?" said the detective. "Is she available?"

Indeed she was. Jeanette entered the kitchen from the dining room, where she must have been hovering with Erica. After the detective lieutenant introduced himself they sat at the kitchen table, where coffee was provided by Erica. "I'm sorry I have to put you through this, Mrs. Casewait," said Morris, "but there are some things about your husband's business affairs that we find puzzling."

"I don't know if I can help you much there," said Jeanette. "After my husband opened his own agency, he seldom confided in me. No office gossip or scandals or things like that, which he was always interested in before."

Since he probably precipitated most of them, thought Henry.

"Did you ever meet any of his business associates or clients, or any of his office staff?" asked Morris.

"No," she said. "As you probably know, I left my husband about six months ago, but our relationship had been deteriorating for some time before that. In fact, we barely spoke to each other. As for his clients or associates, all I remember is a few late night calls, but I didn't overhear anything, if that's what you mean."

Detective Lieutenant Morris duly noted this in his little notebook as he had scrupulously noted everything else, not to give undue significance to any one piece of information, Henry supposed. Either that or he had the worst memory in the world.

"And his office staff?" asked the detective.

"I really don't know if he had any," she answered. "When he left his old job—to be perfectly frank, he was fired—I supposed that he had taken his secretary with him when he went out on his own. That's what they usually do, I believe"—"They," Henry knew, being that vast army of unemployed advertising executives who, even when reduced to complete inactivity and penury, still feel the need for clerical assistance. "But she—his old secretary—called here one day to straighten out some insurance or retirement plan or something, so I guess she had stayed in her old job. So for all I know he didn't even have a secretary."

God, what a fall! thought Henry. For the first time he felt a twinge of compassion for Casewait.

"Why was your husband fired, Mrs. Casewait? If you don't mind telling me, that is?" asked Morris. Henry wondered if the detective lieutenant might be straying outside the limits of permissible inquiry. Perhaps Jeanette should seek some legal advice. But for what? She was in the clear; it was he, Henry, who needed a lawyer.

"My husband was a very difficult man to get along with, especially when he had been drinking. Which was quite often," Jeanette admitted, although, to her credit, reluctantly. "He had almost a compulsion to insult people to their faces, and I imagine he did it once too often, either to his superiors or his coworkers. He had no time at all for those he considered beneath him."

"Would you say that he had made enemies at his old job?"

"I don't know if you'd call them enemies, but he was disliked, I gather, by just about everyone."

Amen to that, thought Henry. He felt sorry for Casewait's former "coworkers" (somehow that term seemed incongruous to Henry, summoning up a picture of shirt-sleeved copywriters and art directors feverishly preparing roughs and layouts instead of lounging at expensive restaurants); they would all probably be questioned by the police, and facing that prospect how many recovering alcoholics wouldn't topple off the wagon, poor devils.

Detective Lieutenant Morris went on to question Jeanette on domestic matters: servants, clubs, debts, entertainment, and the like. "By the way, Mrs. Casewait, has your daughter been notified?" he asked.

"Oh, my God!" exclaimed Jeanette. "How long has it been since we called? She must have arrived at her hotel by now." She briefly explained to Morris the result of their call to Paris.

"Oh?" said Morris. "At what time was that?"

"About one o'clock," said Henry. "If I know the phone company we'll get the precise time on our bill."

"Well, I'm sure she'll be calling soon," said Jeanette. "Oh, how I dread that."

It was now ten o'clock, and Henry remembered guiltily that he had not done a bit of work since the day before yesterday. He began to long for the familiar feel of his typewriter keys and to look forward to returning to the fairly simple problems of McMurdoo and Clagen. It struck him that here before him in the person of the rather aristocratic Lieutenant Morris was a genuine detective. He wondered how McMurdoo would have handled this investigation. To begin with, he would have given Jeanette the once-over and imagined how she would be in bed. Henry looked closely at Morris and had the distinct feeling that in a rather more subtle way than would McMurdoo, he was giving Jeanette the once-over and imagining how she would be in bed.

"Could I help you out?" said Morris. "Unfortunately, the police are rather good at breaking bad news."

Henry felt that he could honestly express an opinion here, but once again elected to remain silent.

"No," said Jeanette, "no, I think I'd better do it myself." She gave Morris an appraising look that was not at all unfavorable. "Thank you just the same. That was very kind of you."

At this point, as if on cue, the phone rang. Erica answered it and then motioned to Jeanette, who hurried over to the phone. "Yes, yes," she said, "this is she."

With considerable tact, Detective Lieutenant Morris rose, and saying, "And now, Mr. Wilnot, could I have one more word with you?" led Henry out of the kitchen and into the front room. "Excuse me," said the detective lieutenant, "but I thought it might be better to let her talk to her daughter alone."

"Of course," said Henry, mildly irritated with Erica, who was still seated at the kitchen table, eagerly anticipating one of those emotional family scenes European women, especially, seem to dote on.

"I also thought I'd take the opportunity to give you this," said Morris, handing Henry an envelope. "As I told you over the phone, we found it with Mr. Casewait's papers."

Henry opened the envelope, which bore his name and was unsealed, and quickly scanned the brief, typewritten note:

Henricus Scriblerus: Dear old friend, if you are reading this it means I have gone west, as they used to say in the trenches. No doubt I have been done in, if not by the booze than by one of the citizenry. If the latter is the case, I hope you will play Holmes to the local Lestrade and assist him in his fumbling efforts, as I have always admired your deductive powers as bodied forth in your shamuses, who usually think with their fists but occasionally with their brains. I am serious. You know me as much as any man; lately more, as I have fallen out with polite society. As coexecutor (surprise!—I *did* get your okay, remember?) you may find out some more. When you speak of it, and you will speak of it, please be kind. Look after Jeanette and Jane and try not to let the lawyers rob them completely blind. They're both bricks, of course, but I wouldn't trust Jeanctte to sort laundry, and Jane has always been distant. In fact, I don't think the girl likes me very much. Well, *ave atque vale*, as the half crazed Wop used to say. To repay you for any good turn you may do my shade, you may have my Loeb Classics. As ever, Joe.

The note was undated.

Henry refolded the paper and put it back into the envelope. Detective Lieutenant Morris was watching him with a bemused expression on his face. He had obviously read the note, thought Henry, and was waiting for a reaction. Henry decided not to give him one; he'd rather think about the note for a while before discussing it. It had revealed one thing very clearly, however, despite the bantering tone: Casewait had known that he was in danger, that someone was out to do him harm.

"May I keep this?" asked Henry. "Or is it part of the record?"

"No, no keep it," said Morris, holding up his hand, palm forward, as though declining a second glass of sherry. "It's just a copy."

They both now turned their attention to the kitchen, where Jeanette was winding up what seemed to be a fairly practical discussion of travel arrangements. "I'll meet you at the airport. . . . No, I insist. It will give me something to do. I still think you should take the Concorde, though. . . . All right, I understand. . . . Yes. See you then." She hung up with a sigh of relief and, turning to Henry and Morris, who were reentering the kitchen, said, "She took it very well, thank God. She'd just gotten in from Charles de Gaulle and our message was waiting for her. She was frantic, and when I told her she seemed almost relieved; she thought it might be me." She paused. "That sounds terrible, doesn't it, but sometimes I think that Jane and I were closer than a natural mother and daughter."

"Natural?" said Morris.

"I'm Jane's stepmother," said Jeanette.

Out came the notebook. "No one told me this. Casewait was married previously?"

"Yes," said Henry, "and you never asked."

"Where is his first wife?" asked Morris.

"She died when Jane was about five. That would be about twenty or twenty-one years ago," said Jeanette. "She died in a car accident," she added, anticipating Morris's next question. "Right around here somewhere."

The detective noted all of this meticulously. "Could you give me her name and the location of the accident? If not now, a little later, perhaps, after you've had time to sort things out," he said considerately. Or not so considerately, thought Henry. It seemed to him that Detective Lieutenant Morris was reserving for himself a great deal of time in their company.

"Didn't you find any of this in Casewait's papers?" asked Henry.

"Not a thing," said Morris. "Of course, it did happen some time ago." He thought to himself awhile and then said abruptly, "Well, I guess that's enough questions for now. Mrs. Casewait, could you come over to your house for a few minutes? We'd like you to look the place over and let us know if you notice anything unusual or out of the way. There's just the chance that you would spot something that we might have missed."

"Do I *have* to?" wailed Jeanette, but it was obvious that she would comply. "Can you give me a few minutes to get ready? I slept late, and now this call from Jane. . . "

"Of course," said Morris. "Mr. Wilnot and I will meet you over there in half an hour, if that's enough time."

"You want me to come?" said Henry, who was beginning to feel the pull of his typewriter stronger than ever. His schedule was already in disarray.

"If you don't mind. We'd like you to look around again. And since you're also coexecutor—or will be, as soon as the original of the will is located—you might as well familiarize yourself with his papers and things. I'm sure the probate court won't mind."

What's this? thought Henry. Probate? What was he getting into? "Of course," he said, deciding to keep his own counsel until he had hired one.

"And besides," said the detective. "You might learn something."

6

As he and Detective Lieutenant Morris walked across the lawn toward the scene of the crime, Henry noticed that a large van was parked in the drive of Casewait's house. "What's that?" he asked.

"The sheriff's mobile crime lab," said Morris. "The pride of the county."

"Is that what all the fuss is about every election year?"

"Yes," said Morris. "It's quite an expensive thing to maintain. The people who make the budget have fits. That's why the sheriff's department tries to use it as much as possible. They'll lend it to any police department in the county. Whether they need it or not," he added. "It's been known to show up at traffic accidents."

"There's something I don't understand here," said Henry as they stopped to contemplate the van. "Yesterday when I discovered the body I called the local police and a sergeant showed up. Then shortly afterward the sheriff came and took charge. And now you show up and seem to be in charge. What I want to know is, who's running this show?"

"Well," said the detective lieutenant, "the crime was committed in this township, which has a police department large enough to handle anything short of a mass prison breakout, which means that we are in charge of the investigation. If there's any part of it we can't handle—we don't have a medical examiner, for instance—the county provides it."

"Just like that?" asked Henry. "For free?"

"Don't worry," said Morris, "everything is paid for in the end, out of taxes. Some towns are so small that they can't afford a police force, or it just doesn't make sense for them to maintain one, so they contract with the sheriff's department to provide law enforcement. Some towns even contract with the state police." He gazed thoughtfully into the middle distance. "It's very interesting sometimes when a crime is committed in an area that lies on the border between the sheriff's territory and the state police's territory. Naturally, some people literally do not know whom to call in an emergency. We sometimes get calls from people two or three townships away. They do their shopping here, you see, and we're the only police they ever see."

"Yes, I know," said Henry. "About the calls, I mean. I sometimes have difficulty getting through."

Detective Lieutenant Morris chose to overlook the remark. "Here," he continued, "we have enough men and facilities to handle this case. Oh, we'll use the county for ballistics or something like that if we need it. Of course, we don't refuse the use of the van, but we could get along without it. If we should happen to run into something we just couldn't handle because of the expense, or something extremely technical, for instance, we'd call on the sheriff's department to take over."

"I see," said Henry. "Then it's like the English system, where the local constabulary calls on the Yard to help them out?"

"God no!" said Morris. "Can you imagine an appointed official like a police chief going to his town board and saying he's stumped and that they'd better call in an *elected* official of the county? The only time this country had anything like the English system was when the FBI still had credibility. Any police chief felt safe in announcing that this was a case for the FBI, even if it wasn't remotely connected with a federal crime. It was his way of saying he was stumped, but it was safe and somehow honorable, and his board or whoever had appointed him would more often than not sympathize with him. Those days are gone, however," he added—wistfully, thought Henry.

"Well, in spite of all the politics, it seems that most crimes get solved—around here, anyway," said Henry, trying to cheer the lieutenant up. And it was true, Henry had to admit. When it came to crimes of violence particularly the county had a remarkable record of arrests and convictions.

"It's usually pretty simple stuff," said Morris. "Murder is sometimes the easiest thing to handle. It's hardly ever premeditated, and if it is the murderer usually breaks down immediately when you question him. There are very few cool, calculating killers around, no matter what you read."

"But what if you don't get to question the killer?" asked Henry.

"If it was premeditated, the murderer must have known the victim, right? So you question everyone the victim knew, regardless of their alibi or their seeming innocence. The murderer's bound to be among them. Then you wait to see which one falls apart. But you question *everyone*, several times, if necessary."

"But what about these random murders you read so much about lately, murders between strangers."

"Yes, I know," said the lieutenant. "That's what has us all worried. You used to be able to predict fairly certainly that a murder was committed by a member of the family; if not, then by a friend or a business associate." Henry noticed that the lieutenant was thoughtful enough not to include neighbors. "We can't do much about maniacs or sex fiends or drug addicts, except follow textbook procedures and hope there were some witnesses or nice obvious clues, or just something stupid done by the killers. You know, a lot of these juvenile-gang types go around afterward *bragging* that they strangled and raped some eighty-year-old woman. Luckily—for us, at least—most of these random killers aren't overloaded with brains."

"What do you think we have here, Lieutenant?"

"I don't know yet. There doesn't seem to be any family involvement, so that means we have to look into his acquaintances—I gather he had few friends—and his business affiliations."

It occurred to Henry that the lieutenant was talking to him rather freely. And wasn't it a truism, of your standard *roman policier* at least, that a detective never told a suspect more than necessary, and that what he *did* tell him was for a purpose? Now, why was Morris telling him all of this, and what wasn't he telling him?

"Then you don't think there's any mystery here?" asked Henry.

"None at all," said the lieutenant. "It's just a killing and will probably be solved by routine methods. For instance, right now my two sergeants are questioning every household on Hardstone Road east of here as far as the parkways, on the chance that somebody might have seen a vehicle, any vehicle, traveling east around seven twenty on the morning of the murder."

Henry was skeptical. "If you depended on me for any information like that, you'd be out of luck. Cars pass by here all day long, and I wouldn't notice one unless it drove up on my lawn, which wouldn't hurt it much. The lawn, I mean." They both looked sadly at Henry's lawn.

"No," said the lieutenant, returning to his theme. "Look at it this way. The only people who travel Hardstone Road that early in the morning are commuters going to the station. The station's west of here, and there's a seven twenty-six train, so any commuter who lives this far away probably would leave his home at seven ten at the latest. This means that at seven twenty westbound traffic would be practically nonexistent. Now, there isn't any industry or any sort of business east of here, so no one would be going to work in that direction. And tradesmen, delivery men, and repairmen don't work that early, right? So the car you heard take off from the front of your house had the road to itself. Suppose it was a foreign car, and a foreign-car buff happened to be looking out his window? Chances are he could describe it perfectly. Or suppose the car was something unusual, like a minibus or one of those new pickups? You'd be surprised what people notice about cars. Whenever I buy a new car, I become intensely aware of every other new car of that make on the road. You see?"

"I suppose you're right," said Henry, who according to his children had not bought a new car within living memory. But he still felt that there was an air of mystery about the case—he was beginning to think of it as a "case" instead of a crime or a murder. After all, he had seen Casewait staggering from his back door, a scene that had begun to rerun itself in his mind in slow motion, in the manner of every known living film director; he had heard the car door slam and the sudden acceleration of the wheels, he had entered the quiet and strangely spotless house, and the whole thing seemed to him . . . well, mysterious.

As they approached the front door of Casewait's house, a policeman in plain clothes came through the open door and down the front steps. He was carrying what looked like a salesman's sample bag. A murder bag? thought Henry, thrilled.

"We're all finished, Lieutenant," said the man. "We'll send you any results, and you know where to reach us if you need us." He seemed hopeful that they would be needed.

"See you, Frank," said Morris. "Tell the sheriff we'll get in touch the minute we feel we can use you."

"Thanks, Lieutenant. I appreciate that," the man said with the air of someone who was just a step away from returning to the suburban equivalent of pounding a beat in the sticks.

"Why don't you just look around?" said the lieutenant to Henry as they entered the silent house. "The place is practically yours now, until you dispose of it."

This would take some getting used to, thought Henry. He felt like asking if that meant mowing the lawn, too. The house looked the same as it had the day before, except for some slight disarrangement of the furniture, as if its exact placement had been left up to movers. Henry looked for signs of fingerprint dust on the furniture but couldn't detect any. He wandered into Casewait's study, a comfortable room with a large mahogany desk and one of those seating affairs that always reminded Henry of a dentist's chair. There was also a large leather reading-smoking chair, good heavy brass lamps, and a side table containing a pipe rack and humidor.

The walls were taken up almost entirely with bookshelves. Casewait had a first-rate library, which had always surprised anyone who had strayed into this room, most likely to escape from his pugnacious and insulting host. Henry had constantly to remind himself that Casewait was an educated, although not cultured, man: it seemed that Casewait had somehow failed to understand the concept of *virtu*, that was all. To him it must have meant something like macho. His education had been along the lines of the British middle class: good prep school, where he learned all that he had needed, and then four years of carousing and making contacts at university. Not a bad system actually, thought Henry, but it had been known to produce some thoroughly bad eggs, on both sides of the Atlantic.

Henry went immediately to the largest bookcase, which took up most of one of the inner walls of the study. There, in the exact center of the ceiling-to-floor array of unclassified books, gleamed an almost perfect square of red spines with bright gold lettering. No fewer than thirty Loeb's Classics—the *old* Loeb's Classics, with real cloth binding and leaf stamping—were stacked on three shelves, making a striking arrangement. Henry doubted there was an interior decorator in the world who could think of such a thing, much less carry it out. It was like a painting; a little light bulb with a metal shade should be placed just above it, or it should be framed, thought Henry. Casewait had inherited the books, and most likely the idea for their arrangement, from his father, who for a time in his youth had been a classics teacher before being left a bundle, as Casewait had put it, by some dotty old aunt who owned a chauffeur-driven limousine of a vintage so rare that collectors had been known to chase after it in the streets. "Christ," Casewait used to say, "I wish she'd left the old man that car. Then maybe he'd have had something better to leave me than these goddamn books."

The titles of the Loebs were a mixed lot, with no apparent focus or preference as to authors or periods; the assemblage of a collector rather than a classicist. Henry had long lusted after them, and now they were his. This was one gift not even Casewait could sully with his cracks about shamuses, and Henry accepted it gratefully.

"You're welcome to run through his papers any time," said Morris, entering the study. "We're through with them. They're in that bottom drawer of the desk—in remarkably good order, I might add."

"Hello? Anybody here?" said Jeanette from the front door. She spoke in a voice hardly louder than her normal speaking voice, perhaps out of respect for her late husband, or in awe of his nonexistence. In the old days her voice would have rung to the rafters, probably with imprecations directed to her errant spouse.

"Ah, Mrs. Casewait," said Morris, nearly breaking a leg to get out of the study and into the front room. "Thank you for coming. I mean, thank you for taking the time. This is, after all, your house." It appeared to Henry that the detective lieutenant was losing his composure. Jeanette had changed into a smart cream-colored pants suit that did nothing to conceal her figure, which seemed a bit trimmer than it used to be to Henry, who had always considered it attractively billowy. Henry had forgotten how young she was; her years with Casewait must have aged her considerably, but she was obviously now recovered.

"Now if you'll just look around for yourself," continued Morris, "or with Mr. Wilnot, I'll be making some phone calls."

Jeanette gave him an interesting look. "Why, thank you, Lieutenant," she said graciously.

"Get a load of this place," said Henry as he and Jeanette began their tour. "Did you ever think that Joe would keep it this neat?"

"Hmm," said Jeanette. "I noticed it immediately. You mean this is the way it looked when . . . when you found him?"

"Well, it's what we found when we came inside for the first time. I was never in here after you left, you know, and I had terrible visions of what it would look like. This turned out to be quite a surprise. As far as I know, he didn't have a housecleaner."

"Actually, you know," said Jeanette, "it isn't all that great. Look at the windows." Henry knew what she meant. Where the sunlight touched them, they showed a generous coating of grime.

"The furniture has been dusted, and the silver's been touched up," continued Jeanette, casting an appraising eye around the house, "but I don't see much more than a run through with the carpet sweeper and a good session with the dishwasher. I'll bet the hampers are full and the sheets need changing." She was right. The hampers in the laundry room and in both bathrooms were full, and the beds, particularly the double bed in the master bedroom, proved to have well-used sheets and pillowcases beneath the pristine counterpanes. Since Casewait hadn't had any houseguests, at least as far as Henry knew, it looked as though he had slept in each bed in each bedroom in tandem. Now *that* seemed more like Casewait's style.

"Still," said Henry, "*someone* fixed this place up, even if it isn't as neat as it looks." To him it had seemed gleaming, but then, since his children had left home, he took merely the absence of clothing strewn on the floor to indicate spotlessness.

They continued their tour of the house, uncovering more evidence of Casewait's lack of household skills. His closet was a scandal, and the drawers of his dresser didn't seem to have any system at all. Socks were thrown in with shirts and pajamas, and nothing seemed to be folded except new purchases that had not been taken out of their wrappings yet. Henry thought he detected the evidence of a man who solved his laundry problems by buying new shirts and linens as he ran out of the old. They would probably discover a huge cache of unclaimed laundry at one of the local cleaners soon.

"Oh, Henry," moaned Jeanette, "I really don't feel up to this. I just want to get back to California and take up my real life again. I hate to ask you to take all this on, but maybe you and Jane, when she gets here, can take care of, well, clearing up. Jane's got a good head on her shoulders; she can be my agent or whatever."

Henry wasn't so sure about that—Jane's having a good head on her shoulders. Running away to join the maharishis did not lead Henry's list of examples of levelheadedness. However, he recalled Jane as an earnest and serious person who usually saw a task through, be it constructing a near perfect compost heap or helping Henry's son set up his electrical musical apparatus.

"Of course," said Henry, "we'll take care of everything, or if we can't, we'll get someone who can. Lieutenant," he said to Morris, who had entered the kitchen, where they were now standing, "what's next? Mrs. Casewait would like to return to her home and job in California. Is it absolutely necessary that she stay here much longer?"

"I'll stay until Jane arrives, of course," Jeanette put in hurriedly, probably not wanting to give the impression that she was abandoning ship completely.

"Well," said Morris, "I was just talking on the phone with Chief Desplaines and he says that the medical examiner has definitely ruled that your husband died as the result of foul play and the police are charged to find the—ah, sorry, perpetrator of the crime. Or perpetrators," he added, whether significantly or otherwise Henry could not tell.

"Will there be an inquest or anything like that?" asked Henry, whose knowledge of legal and police procedure came almost exclusively from British mystery novels. None of Henry's private eyes ever had anything to do with such matters. They just took a case, tracked down the killer, had the living hell beat out of them at least once, then in turn beat the living hell out of the killer and/or his henchmen, and handed the whole package over to the police or the DA.

"We have a grand jury system here," said Morris. "The medical examiner determines if there has been a crime, the police gather evidence and hand it over to the district attorney, who presents it to the grand jury, which decides if anyone should be charged and turned over for trial. Simple. Of course, we're pretty sure of our case before we turn it over to the DA; and he's pretty sure of his case before he takes it to the grand jury. Or should be," he added, again with that wistful look on his face that Henry had noticed before.

"But Jeanette won't be needed for that, will she?"

"No, I suppose not. In fact, so far you and the medical examiner are the only people we now have who could tell the grand jury anything."

"You mean *I'll* have to testify," said Henry, several Perry Mason reruns immediately unreeling in his mind.

"If you do, it will probably only be to answer a few basic questions," said Morris, "not a petit jury trial where you have to face a defense counsel. Most cases never get to trial anyway."

"Oh, dear," said Jeanette. "I didn't realize all *that* could happen. I do hope you don't mind too much, Henry."

"Oh, no," said Henry, who *did* mind, but what could he do? He felt that he was being drawn inexorably into a veritable maelstrom of uncontrollable events, as Hamilton Burger would have put it.

"We'll wait till Jane gets here before we make any plans,"

said Jeanette. "Right now I'd just like to get out of this *place*. Excuse me, Lieutenant. I'll see you later, Henry."

"Look, Lieutenant," said Henry as Jeanette sailed out the back door, not unwatched by the interested constable, he noted. "Lieutenant?" he repeated.

"Oh, yes," said Morris, not taking his eyes off Jeanette—or at least, part of her—until she was completely out of sight.

"Just what do I do now?"

"I suggest you get in touch with Casewait's lawyer or your own lawyer. First you'll have to get hold of the original will, and then some letters testamentary from the surrogate's court, and—"

"Wait a minute," interrupted Henry. "What are letters testamentary and what's a surrogate's court?"

"Just papers that give you the go-ahead to settle the estate. I take it you're going to do the executor's job here; Mrs. Casewait doesn't seem to want any part of it, and you were specifically named in the will."

"And surrogate's court?"

"That's a probate court, handles wills and things."

"Why isn't it called a probate court then?"

"I don't know," said Morris.

Fair enough, thought Henry. There was no need to pursue some things too deeply. You might sink in over your head and never get out. "How do I start this whole chain of events?" asked Henry.

"Actually, you can't do a thing until you receive the death certificate signed by the medical examiner. It should be ready by now, and I'll see that copies are sent over to you. If I don't bring them myself," he added. And get another eyeful of Jeanette, thought Henry. He had the feeling that Detective Lieutenant Morris was going to be popping by fairly frequently from now until Jeanette departed for her native heath.

"In the meantime," continued Morris, I'd familiarize myself with Casewait's affairs. You might just have a job ahead of you." He motioned toward the study. "As I said, you're completely free to start going through his papers."

7

HENRY HAD ONCE seen a movie version of *Madama Butterfly* in which Japanese and American actors played the dramatic roles while stars of the Italian opera supplied the voices, all under the supervision of a Japanese art director and American film and sound technicians. The idea was to demonstrate what marvelous things could happen when American technology was wedded to Italian musicality and Japanese taste. The high point arrived early in the film with Butterfly's entrance through what seemed a curtain of pink and white blossoms. The actress playing Butterfly was an incredibly tiny, porcelainlike figure, but when she opened her mouth, out came the voice of a two-hundred-pound Italian supersoprano. The audience was astonished. "Christ," said a hushed voice in the darkness. "That Jap can *sing*!"

After his first rapid survey of Casewait's personal papers, Henry had something of the same feeling. Not only could this particular Jap sing but had probably designed the sets and rehearsed the orchestra. Henry could only wish that his own affairs were in such perfect order as Casewait's. Here was everything, the surface record of a life: checking accounts, savings accounts, brokerage accounts, income tax returns, insurance policies, mortgage payments, even a listing of personal property—Henry noticed that the Loeb Classics were evaluated at five hundred dollars, a very modest and conservative sum—all in labeled envelopes neatly arranged in alphabetical order. But, as with the singing Jap, suspicion soon set in: the lip sync wasn't all it should be, and there were no deep breaths between passages that would render a normal person unconscious. It seemed to Henry that Casewait had been expecting an audit.

It is said that, next to his sex life, the most intriguing thing about a man is his financial condition—and forget about his health! Henry was of an age where he couldn't care less about anyone's sex life, including his own, but let him peek at a man's bank balance and he became at once alive to the human condition in all its mystery and joy—not to mention its pity and sorrow, as in his own case. It turned out that Casewait had been a bit better off than Henry had supposed. The house alone was worth more than two hundred seventy-five thousand and was just about paid for. Savings accounts and checking accounts contained about six thousand, and saving certificates and bonds were worth another twenty thousand. There was also a brokerage account that amounted to almost fifteen thousand; investments brought in about six thousand a year. There was no trust account, Henry noted. He had always supposed that Casewait had inherited his money, and, though squandering most of it, must have provided something for his daughter. But there was no trace of Jane here, except for a loan for college expenses some years back, which apparently had been paid off. By whom? Jane? If so, Henry was at once revolted by the idea of Casewait's making his only child pay for her own education and moved to reluctant admiration for a man who could pull it off. His own children, having picked his carcass clean, were still toying with the bones.

Henry could not find any business records among the papers in the desk and concluded that they must be kept in Casewait's office; he reflected with a sinking heart that this would mean contacting Casewait's accountant. Now, accountants as a class did not bother Henry too much—after all, what would the workaday world do without them—but it was as individuals that he found them insufferable. To forestall having even to think about this, he made a telephone call to Scanlon, the reluctant activist.

"What can I do for you?" said Scanlon when he came on

the line after only a slight delay. "How's it going? Big Sam got you tied in with the Mafia yet?"

"What?" said Henry.

"The Mafia," said Scanlon. "Big Sam's got this thing about them. He's convinced that they run the county and he sees them everywhere, particularly around election time. I'll bet you anything he's decided that this murder of yours is the work of a hit man."

"Hmm," said Henry. "You know, it just might be. The police think the murder gun had a silencer, and your garden-variety murderer doesn't carry a gun with a silencer."

"Well, if it is, it'll be the first time—that Sam's uncovered the Mafia, that is. How's it going otherwise?" Henry explained his involvement as coexecutor. "Anybody going to contest the will?" asked Scanlon.

"No, there's just the wife and daughter involved, and they're not about to dispute anything."

"So what's your problem?"

"Well, what do I do next?"

"You file the will for probate," said Scanlon, who sounded a bit irritated. He probably had more useful things to do, thought Henry, like pleading the inalienable rights of privileged youth.

"Look," said Scanlon, "I can't help you with this myself, but somebody in my office will be in touch with you. How's the family fixed for cash?"

"All right, I guess. They both must have credit cards, I imagine."

"Good. It may take a few days to get into—what's his name?—Casewait's checking or savings accounts. Do you know who his lawyer was?"

"His name is Roscoe Van Dam." This name was well known in the area. It belonged to a family so old and full of lawyers that it was purported its earliest member had represented absentee patroons in grievances against the Dutch West India Company. This ancestor's specialty had been obtaining compensation for losses resulting from Indian attacks. It was said by his detractors, who were mostly Englishmen from Connecticut, and biased, that his real specialty was *staging* Indian attacks with the willing compliance of any Mohawks who happened to be passing through the Hudson Valley.

"He's retired," said Henry, referring to the present Van Dam, "but his office may still be in business. I'll find out."

"Great. Just give everything to my associate when she shows up. Listen, I gotta run. A couple of these rotten little rich bastards came back from a cruise loaded with so much stuff that they had to get rid of some of it, so they took it. The boat was slow in docking so one of them decided to walk ashore. I gotta spring him as soon as they finish pumping him out. Jesus, where will it all end?" he said good-naturedly and hung up.

Henry felt a little better, although Scanlon had not yet given him any reason to think that he was in capable hands. He decided to take a break from Casewait's affairs. Could he get a little work in? He wandered into the kitchen and peered out the back window. He could see a corner of his own work shed through the trees. He was drawn to it. He stepped out the back door, but then he realized that he was retracing Casewait's last erratic journey. Directly before him lay the loathsome swimming pool, recently drained by Morris's minions. What had they been looking for, he wondered.

He mounted the platform from which he had fished the unfortunate Casewait and pondered once again whatever had possessed the man to install it. More than once Casewait had complained to Henry about the cost and effort of upkeep. But perhaps that had been the point. How many times had the affluent advised Henry against a course of action he had never contemplated in the first place? "Henry, never buy a Rolls-Royce," he had once been told by a man at a cocktail party. "More trouble than they're worth, more trouble than they're worth," he had muttered to himself, wandering off to the kitchen to advise the maid not to sink all of her money into offshore oil stocks. In exactly the same vein, Casewait had once said, "Henry, never buy a swimming pool. You're smart, stay away from them. My god, the draining, the cleaning, the chlorine—you wouldn't believe it!" And with that he had thrown himself into the water and begun making his odious seal-barking sounds while Henry stood at the edge of the pool with his brown bag lunch and his thermos of coffee on his way to his humble work shed, which was intended to house a horse.

Henry paused beside the compact grouping of machinery that serviced the pool. He hadn't the slightest idea of what was what, but he recognized a tank that led to a hose that led to an opening in the platform and thence to the pool. The filtering system, he thought. There was a lock mechanism where the hose attached to the tank, and a key protruded from the lock, rather loosely, it seemed to Henry. He turned the key to see what would happen, maliciously hoping that water would spurt from some unseen source and engulf the whole dreadful structure and sweep it down the slight slope it was perched on.

Nothing happened; in fact, the key didn't even engage the lock. Henry tried to insert it in the lock, but it just did not fit. He tried it again, but it still did not fit. Could Morris's people have left it in the wrong lock? He looked around the pool and even descended and investigated under the platform, but he could not find any other locking device. As he emerged from beneath the walkway, he heard a rustling in the surrounding woods. He pocketed the key guiltily, half expecting Harley or Bierson to leap on him from the bushes and accuse him of pilfering evidence. The woods resumed their silence, however, and he assumed that the noise he had heard was made by one of his friends, the deer, who roamed the environs freely. Whatever it was, though, it had sounded big, and Henry moved with some alacrity across Casewait's lawn and onto his own property.

Ahead lay his workshop, which he gratefully gained, spending the rest of the day staring at a blank sheet of paper in his typewriter, completely blocked.

Jane arrived the following afternoon. She surprised them by taking a limousine from the airport to the local Hilton, or Statler, or Holiday Inn, or Howard Johnson, or whichever chain happened to own the structure at the time, and a cab from there. Henry thanked her sincerely for this, since trips to the airports serving the city were high on his list of things to be avoided at all costs.

Jane Casewait was a favorite of Henry's. His own daughter, Gretchen, had long since drifted away to schools and to a sort of perpetual hiking trip through Europe where she seemed to be circling in ever-decreasing circles on Stuttgart, the home of her maternal grandparents. Comforting her old dad in his dotage was definitely not one of her priorities. Jane, on the other hand, had for most of her life stayed close to home. Henry could remember her as a young girl helping him with his gardening or dropping around to visit him in his work shed, a lonely but enchanting child. When it had come time for her to go away to school, she had simply turned her back on her house and parents and had been rarely seen since. An attraction to transcendental meditation and yoga were really not too farfetched in Jane's case, when one thought about it. She had always had a rather chilling self-sufficiency, and those two disciplines—if one could call them that—would naturally appeal to a young woman who had more or less been fending for herself since her mother had died. Casewait, of course, had never had much time for her and had not been worried or surprised when her schooling turned into what appeared to be a permanent studentship. Her mother had wisely set up a trust for her from her family's money, so Jane was probably better off than your average maharishi's housekeeper.

"Hello, Mr. Wilnot," she said after the first flurry of greetings to and from Jeanette and Erica. Henry did not mind her mode of address; he knew that she was no more capable of calling him Henry than the late Lyndon B. Johnson was of pronouncing Venezuela.

"Hello, Janey, good to see you again," he said. And it was. She had perfectly straight blond hair to her shoulders, and the well-scrubbed look that used to be the mark of graduates of expensive northeastern girls' schools. Her features were as regular as any soap-commercial model's, but her blue eyes radiated intelligence rather than warmth. She was wearing a loose-fitting maroon pants suit of a soft, full material that nearly concealed the built-up left shoe and the twiglike left arm, several inches shorter than the right one. Henry never saw these deformities without experiencing a slight lurch of his whole moral platform. Everything he believed in was knocked slightly out of kilter. If this could happen, he thought, then nothing was to be ruled out. He would have gladly given her his arm and his leg in exchange for those pitiful and imperfect limbs.

Jane had been born prematurely and malformed. No one cared to admit it, but the cause had been some morning sickness pills that Casewait had obtained in Europe while on a business trip. His wife's agony was driving him crazy, he had said, and everybody over there was taking them. He swore they weren't Thalidomide; if they were the damage would have been much greater. And anyway, it couldn't be proved that the pills were to blame; Jane had been born prematurely. It was after hearing this that Henry's slumbering dislike for Casewait began to quicken.

"How was the flight?" asked Henry after they had all been supplied with the obligatory coffee and snacks. "Did you get a seven forty-seven?"

"It wasn't bad," said Jane. "Yes, I guess it was a seven forty-seven, and we left Charles de Gaulle at twelve o'clock. The movie was terrible."

"Oh, I wish you had taken the Concorde," said Jeanette. "You're going to have terrible jet lag."

"I'd rather have jet lag than get on one of those things," said Jane. "They really scare me. Even the little sixteen-seater I took from Lyon to Paris is safer, if you ask me. That's why I wasn't at my hotel when you called, by the way. We had to land at Dijon to let off some fat-cat businessman and weren't allowed to take off again for hours."

"Tell us all about what you've been doing," said Erica.

"Wait a minute," said Henry. "Maybe Jane would like to know the schedule, what we've been doing and have to do, and all that."

"Of course, dear," said Erica. "How stupid of me." Henry as quickly and tactfully as possible told Jane the story of her father's death as he saw fit. He then outlined his responsibilities and actions as coexecutor of the estate.

"I'll try to take this thing as far as I can myself," he told her, "but if it gets to be too much for me I'll have to turn it over to someone else—a lawyer or the bank or both. Now, if you have any objections or reservations, let me know, and I'll make the proper arrangements."

"Don't be silly, Mr. Wilnot," Jane said. "I have complete confidence in you. In fact, I feel much better knowing you'll be looking after things for us."

"How would you like the funeral handled?"

"I haven't the slightest idea," she said. "Jeanette?"

"That nice detective told me that there's a funeral home that does a lot of business with the county and they know . . . well, the procedure in things like this. Anyway, since Joe never said anything about it, or had a cemetery plot or anything, I think he should be cremated."

"You're probably right," said Henry. "How about you, Jane?"

Jane shrugged assent. She seemed quite uninterested. No help there, thought Henry. "Okay, then it's settled," he said, rubbing his hands together for some reason, as though he had just successfully taken orders for a round of drinks rather than disposed of the earthly remains of his former friend and neighbor. "You can stay here, if you like," he said to Jane. "Harold's old room is empty, except for all that electrical gear he used to use in his band. I'll move it."

"Oh, God," said Jane, "I remember that, the band. The din was tremendous. We could hear it even in the wintertime with all the windows shut. What were their names? I've forgotten."

"Harold and the Tribunes," said Henry with a pained expression. "And they're now as defunct as the great newspaper whose name they desecrated. I think disco did them in," he added. "Well, how about it?"

"No, I think I'll stay next door—at home, I mean. God, these things have us all mixed up. But thank you, anyway."

"I'll stay with you," said Jeanette, "at least for tonight. I'm going back to the Coast right after the funeral, if I can. Henry?"

"I don't see why not," said Henry, "but I'll check it out with Morris. I'll also have to get in touch with Scanlon—that's the lawyer I've been consulting—and find out the details of the will and probate. How are you fixed? Financially, I mean. Need any money to tide you over? Scanlon can fix it up."

"Oh, no," said Jeanette. "Don't worry about that. Anyway, I've got enough credit cards to get me through the next fifty years, at least. You know, borrow enough from one to make the minimum payment on the others. A man at the office explained it to me."

Hmm, thought Henry, an interesting idea. He'd have McMurdoo try it in his next caper.

The following morning Henry called Detective Lieutenant Morris and after twelve or fifteen rings was finally connected with someone who sounded like either Harley or Bierson, strengthening his suspicion that they constituted the entire uniformed force of the township. When Morris got on the line he said that it would be all right for Jeanette to return to Los Angeles—did Henry detect a note of regret in his voice?—but she must realize that she could be called back at any time. "But that shouldn't be too much trouble for her, should it?" he said.

"I don't know," said Henry. "Shouldn't it?"

"She lives in Marina del Rey, doesn't she?"

"I guess so," said Henry, confused. He really didn't know where she lived, except in that vast oasis on the other side of several ranges of mountains.

"That's just a hop, skip, and a jump from the L.A. International Airport," explained Morris. Anyway, he continued, she must realize that she would have to keep them informed of her whereabouts if she traveled anywhere, and she should not leave the country. "A standard caveat," said the lieutenant, sounding rather like a former secretary of state.

"I shall make sure that she is properly caveated," said Henry.

"It might also be a good idea for you to get power of attorney from her, or some other instrument of the court that will let you act for her," said Morris. "Your lawyer will know."

"Right," said Henry with alacrity. He was beginning to do things without question. If Morris told him to give himself up and confess to the brutal murder of Joseph Casewait, he would probably cheerfully present himself at the station house for incarceration. After hanging up, Henry dialed Scanlon's number and after the usual questions, evasions, and, for all Henry knew, outright lies, was informed that the noted civil libertarian was in court. "Could you hold on a minute, sir?" said Scanlon's receptionist. "Miss Nathan would like to speak with you."

Henry assented and in a few moments was connected with a pleasant-voiced young woman who explained that she was Mr. Scanlon's associate who would be handling the details involved in the probate of Casewait's will and any other matters that might come up in the settling of the estate. "Mr.

Scanlon feels that we should act as quickly as possible to get things settled before any indictments are handed down."

"Indictments?" said Henry, in a voice pitched higher than he would have wished.

"Well, yes," said Miss Nathan. "The police work rather quickly up your way, and we can only assume that the per—the murderer will be appre—arrested and charged fairly soon." From her tentativeness, Henry guessed that this young lady might have been a peace officer before becoming a lawyer. What she probably *wanted* to say was that the perpetrator would soon be apprehended and if we had our way about it we'd string him up by his nuts. "I have all the papers ready for your signature, so if I could drop by fairly soon, I would appreciate it."

"Thank you," said Henry. "but I was prepared to come by your office. I'd like to see Mr. Scanlon again, for one thing."

"I quite understand," said Miss Nathan. "Everyone does." Henry thought he detected a shade more than the usual adoration that female associates of hotshot male lawyers show for their bosses. "But he really is tied up in a very important proceeding just now, so I'll just drop everything off later this afternoon, if I may. Say about four o'clock?"

"Certainly," said Henry. "I'll be expecting you. And by the way, could you prepare a power of attorney or something that will allow me to act for Mrs. Casewait."

"Oh, yes. I was going to suggest that," she said. "Do you know if Mrs. Casewait plans to remain here in the East or return to California?"

"I'm pretty sure she will return to California permanently. In fact, she's leaving for there as soon as she can. Business and personal reasons, I suppose."

"Well, I ask because that means that you as coexecutor with her power of attorney will be able to dispose of all the property of the estate."

"Yes, I guess so, although I haven't given it much thought."

"I'm thinking primarily of the real estate. Do you plan to rent or sell the Casewait house?"

"Why, sell, of course," said Henry. People in these parts, he might have added, don't *rent* houses. They much prefer to make themselves permanent hostages to them.

"Have you taken any steps in that direction yet?" she asked.

"No, but I know a few real estate people I can get in touch with. There's no particular hurry. The mortgage has nearly been paid off and the taxes aren't due for another five months." How well Henry knew that.

"Well, before you put it on the market, I'd like to talk to you—as a representative of Mr. Scanlon, of course. In the course of our dealings with several clients, we come across many who are anxious to relocate in a rural area but prefer not to work through regular real estate channels."

Oh, oh, thought Henry. Scanlon must be relocating his weirdos in the suburbs. He remembered that bomb factory in the city that blew up, leaving nothing to identify the student-activist occupants except a few fingers and their American Express cards. he was beginning to wonder if he might be better off with another lawyer, like the old duffer who drew up Casewait's will. *He* belonged to the Elks Club.

"Look," said Henry, "I know a little about Mr. Scanlon's clientele—in fact, he told me about them himself—and I really do not have any desire to have them as neighbors."

"Oh, no, Mr. Wilnot," she said, laughing heartily. "This is quite different from the sort of thing Mr. Scanlon has become famous for." Famous? thought Henry, I didn't know he was famous. "We represent many different areas of society, including respectable educators, artists, and scientists who simply do not trust your normal—how can I put it?—housewife, PTA chairperson, station-wagon-driving, part-time real estate saleswoman."

Not a bad description, thought Henry, although these days not many of them could afford to maintain a station wagon.

"Oh, all right," he said. "You might as well look at the house while you're here. Is there anything special I should have ready for you when you come?"

"Well, a copy of the will, of course—it doesn't have to be the original—and you might start working on a list of assets. Also, I'll have to see the lawyer who drew up the will. Is he available?"

"Oh, he's available, all right." If you can call drinking sloe gin fizzes and playing euchre at the Elks Club all day available, thought Henry. "But don't expect much help from him. The day he retired he turned his back on his office and hasn't been there since. Can't say I blame him."

"No problem," said Miss Nathan. "His records must have been taken care of in the usual way; assigned to his partners, or whatever. What I was really worried about was whether he might be a little put out that his firm wasn't hired for the probate."

"No, he couldn't care less, and I understand his two younger partners aren't interested in anything except advancing their own political careers. In fact, about the only time they're in the area is around election time, and then they're too busy standing on train platforms shaking hands and forcing printed matter on commuters to do anything else."

"That settles it, then," said Miss Nathan. "I'll see you around four."

After hanging up, Henry smiled to himself. He hadn't told Miss Nathan that he already had a list of assets, and he looked forward to springing it on her and winning her grudging respect. For some reason, she had struck Henry as someone whom he would like to score points with. He wondered if she was pretty. He also wondered if Casewait's books were on the up-and-up. And where were the business records for his shop, as admen called their usually luxurious offices? They must be with his accountant, he decided, and dismissed the matter from his mind as he headed up the back walk to his work shed.

8

When miss Nathan presented herself at his front door promptly at four o'clock, Henry was mildly pleased and surprised. For one thing, his front door was used so seldom that he had been prepared either for a couple of Jehovah's Witnesses soliciting converts or a confused priest searching for the monasterylike girls' school farther along the road. For another, he had hoped but not expected that Scanlon's colleague would be anything but your run-of-the-mill legal activist with kinky hair down to her shoulders, probably clad in blue jeans and carrying a knapsack in lieu of a briefcase. Miss Nathan turned out to be of medium height with a slender figure and gleaming black hair that just covered her ears, clad in a severe blue *suit* with white blouse and stock, stockings and pumps, and carrying a regulation black briefcase. She also had a pleasant and obviously well-scrubbed and made-up face. Dark, intelligent eyes sized Henry up briefly as she introduced herself. Henry couldn't help straightening up and sucking in his stomach.

They went into the living room and, after an exchange of small talk, got down to business. All of the women were next door, appraising and sorting out Casewait's chattels, so Henry and Miss Nathan were undisturbed.

"Now then, where shall we start?" said Miss Nathan, seating herself on the sofa and crossing one slender leg over another.

When Henry was in the sixth grade, he had had a teacher named Miss Nichols; he never knew her first name because in those days teachers didn't have first names. Henry did not know then what the word *polymath* meant, but he knew in his bones that Miss Nichols was a polymath. She knew everything; from any given French irregular verb to the binomial theorem, she had the number on it. Another remarkable thing about Miss Nichols was that she was good-looking—that is, she didn't look like one's mother, maid, neighbor, or whichever older female acquaintances one had according to one's parents' economic and social status. Miss Nichols was quite simply a knockout. She wore only one outfit, as far as Henry could remember: a white blouse with a ruffled front or stock around the neck, and a severe, slim, elegant knee-length black skirt.

Now, normally in a classroom Henry would be seated along with the rest of the Ws, Ys, and Zs in that Siberia far to the right and rear of the room, but for some reason Miss Nichols took a shine to him—he was a cute little tyke even then—and seated him directly in front of her desk, in the first row. And it so happened that sometime during virtually every class Miss Nichols, tiring of her seated position behind the desk, would get up and walk around to the front of it. There she would continue to lecture, leaning back slightly so that her buttocks (if it could be imagined that Miss Nichols had such things) rested gently against the edge of the desktop. Sometimes she would place the palms of her hands behind her on the desk and ease herself to a sitting position on the desk, her legs dangling over the edge, her knees perhaps two or three centimeters apart. And then, gazing distractedly at the corner of the ceiling or out the window, perhaps trying to recall the exact figure for the annual average rainfall in the Amazon basin, Miss Nichols would quite unselfconsciously lift her skirt an infinitesimal distance above her knees and cross one leg over the other.

It is absurd to suppose that a healthy, active eleven-year-old boy could suffer cardiac arrest, but that is exactly what happened to Henry every time Miss Nichols performed this innocent movement: his heart actually missed a beat. Too young to know what was happening to him and ignorant of the possibility of any physical release, he became a very troubled little boy. Confused, unsure of his feelings, he withdrew within himself and assumed a preoccupied air that was to mark him for the rest of his life.

"Mr. Wilnot?" said Miss Nathan.

"Oh," said Henry, "I'm sorry. What were you saying?"

"I thought we might start with these," she said, handing him various documents for signature, explaining them as she went along. "This is a letter testamentary, which is really the most important in that it gives you the power to act for the deceased, to collect all of his assets and distribute them to his beneficiaries after you have paid all of his debts and collected all of his credits. It gives you the right to deposit into or withdraw moneys from all his accounts and to open his safe deposit boxes, if he has any."

"What about his business debts and credits?" asked Henry.

"Did he own his own business?"

"I really don't know if it was what you'd call a business. He was sort of a freelance and a consultant, but I don't know if he had any clients. He had an office in the city, but I don't know what sort of shape it was in. He hadn't been in business for himself very long."

"Was he incorporated?"

"I don't think so. Maybe he was in the process of doing it, or maybe he was waiting till his business got off the ground. I just don't know."

"Well, if he wasn't, that means that his business has to be treated like any of his other assets and any business debts or credits will have to be treated as personal." she said. "Let's just hope he didn't run up a fortune in expenses."

Henry groaned inwardly. If there was one thing Casewait had been capable of doing it was running up a fortune in expenses. And yet there was his solid financial condition to consider. This point still made Henry uneasy.

"Did he employ anyone else, such as a secretary or accountant?"

"Not that I know of. I called his office but was unable to get an answer. His wife doesn't believe he even had a secretary, which seems unusual for an adman. I assume he had some sort of bookkeeper or accountant, but maybe he employed somebody just part time. You know, somebody who works at home after hours from his regular job." Henry subscribed to the popular notion that accountants worked like beavers, although the ones he knew spent most of their time in Florida.

"Well, I'd certainly find out as soon as I could," said Miss Nathan. "Have you taken an inventory of his office equipment—typewriters, calculators, that sort of thing?"

"No," said Henry, a bit sheepishly. "In fact, I've never been to his office."

Miss Nathan gave him a mildly censorious glance and said, "I can only advise you to get down there as fast as you can and make an inventory and arrange for its disposal or protection. If I know the city, if anyone has heard of Mr. Casewait's death the place will probably be cleaned out by now."

"Go into the city?" said Henry.

"Yes," she said flatly. "I think it is quite important that you do. Mr. Wilnot, you have to realize that you are now responsible for this estate, and if an expensive piece of office equipment that is being leased or is rented disappears, you may have to make it right."

"But surely there would be insurance," said Henry.

"That's what you have to find out, and right away. I'd go in immediately if I were you."

"Into the city?" said Henry.

"Yes," she said firmly. "I realize it's too late to do it today, but I'd try to do it first thing in the morning." She began to pack up her papers. "I'll leave these with you. They're work sheets, lists of requirements, and other aids for probate that

Mr. Scanlon has worked out for clients over the years. I think you'll find them most helpful." At her mention of Scanlon's name, her eyes gleamed with admiration, Henry noted.

"Mr. Scanlon is quite a guy, I take it," he said.

Miss Nathan chose to overlook his slightly snide tone of voice. "Yes, he is," she said evenly, "a *great* man," and finished stuffing her papers into her attaché case.

I'm in the presence of a disciple, thought Henry. But one who's a bit on the defensive, he also noted.

"Now, if you have the time," she said pleasantly, "I'd appreciate it if you'd let me look through Mr. Casewait's house—or *your* house, I should say."

"Of course," said Henry. "My wife and Casewait's wife and daughter are over there now, so I'll just introduce you to them and they'll show you around. My wife and Mrs. Casewait between them probably know more about the house than I do anyway."

"What a charming house *you* have, Mr. Wilnot," Miss Nathan said as he led her into the kitchen toward the back door. "And so well kept up."

"Well," said Henry, "the lawn may leave a little to be desired . . . "

"No, I mean the interior," she said, looking around the kitchen approvingly. "Of course, I don't mean it's not to be expected, but it's just that my work takes me into some pretty grim places, so it's always a pleasure to enter a house so, well, neat and tidy."

"Oh?" said Henry, looking around him. "I hadn't noticed." He had to admit she was right; the old place did look rather nice. He must tell Erica; it was probably the first compliment on her housekeeping she had ever received.

As Henry escorted Miss Nathan across the lawn to Casewait's house he sought to redress the gaffe he had committed by not giving Scanlon the respect his attractive colleague thought his due. "I'd like your advice, Miss Nathan," he said. "Mr. Casewait—the deceased, I mean—owned two huge cars, one a station wagon, and both tremendous gas guzzlers. I'd like to get rid of them as soon as possible. I noticed that the insurance payments are tremendous, not that I intend to renew them." Henry found that he was beginning to think of Casewait's possessions as his own, just as everyone had been telling him they were. "I know that I can't get anywhere near their book value if I try to sell them, but I've heard that if you donate cars to schools, vocational schools or schools for . . . well, wayward boys, *privileged* wayward boys, that is"—Scanlon should know plenty of those, he thought—"I've heard that you can deduct the full book value from your taxes, the estate's taxes, I mean."

Miss Nathan looked at him closely and said, "Of course, Mr. Wilnot, that's a very wise thing to do. I'll be glad to send you the addresses of several institutions that would be delighted to receive them. And it's a good idea to get these big cars off the road."

"Yes, yes, exactly," said Henry, thinking fondly of his ancient Volkswagen and Erica's little Pinto. Somehow, though, he felt that he had lost some sort of advantage to Miss Nathan, and by extension, to Scanlon. Why did he feel this way about what was probably an excellent lawyer and his very competent assistant?

Henry introduced Miss Nathan to Erica and the Casewaits, who eagerly began to show off their home. Miss Nathan, who seemed experienced in these matters, willingly let herself be borne along, and the whole crowd of women were soon tramping up and down stairs and in and out of rooms.

Before returning to his work shed, Henry thought he might have a look at Casewait's cars and check on these instruments of the innocent bit of chicanery he was planning for the tax boys. The garage was semiattached and could be entered by a side door approached through a breezeway. Henry peeked in the window and saw the monstrous Oldsmobile that Casewait had obtained for practically nothing through some agency shenanigans, but the equally gargantuan Ford station wagon was missing. Strange, thought Henry. It seemed to him that he had seen or heard the car recently, and had noted it because Casewait seldom used it, and for obvious reasons, since every time he took it out of the garage the nation's oil reserves were severely depleted. Before leaving, Henry asked Erica if she knew anything about the car's whereabouts; she didn't, but said that she had seen it parked in Casewait's driveway for the past few days. Hmm. Henry supposed that the urbane flatfoot, Detective Lieutenant Morris, should be informed immediately, so upon regaining his kitchen he put through the call and waited for the usual twelve or fifteen rings.

Lieutenant Morris seemed quite interested. "You say your wife saw it parked in the driveway the day before Casewait was shot?" he asked. "That means it's unlikely that he left it at the station or an airport. He didn't sell it, by any chance?"

"There's no record of it if he did," said Henry. "He paid his insurance annually, so I imagine he would have done something about that if he had gotten rid of it."

"Hmm, yes. Could you give me the details—description, license number, registration."

"It was a maroon 1979 Ford Country Squire station wagon, a real monster," said Henry.

"That was a bad year for the Country Squire, wasn't it, what with the oil shortage? Weren't they thinking of discontinuing it?"

"Probably. That would explain how Casewait came by it. He was always picking up new cars through his advertising agency. They all do it—advertising men, I mean. Some distributor probably paid him to take if off his hands." Henry gave the lieutenant the rest of the information he needed.

"We'll put out a check on it," said Morris. "It could have been stolen. You didn't hear anything that night that you haven't mentioned, or maybe forgot?"

"No. It was pretty cool that night and most of our windows were closed. His garage and drive are on the far side of the house from ours, and we've never been able to hear the sound of his cars."

"The car you heard in the morning was toward the front of the house?"

"Yes."

"No chance that the car you heard was the Ford?"

"No, definitely not. The car I heard took off like a racer. The Ford moves like an ocean liner."

"Well," said Morris, "that takes care of that. Thank you very much, Mr. Wilnot, you've been very helpful, and this is most interesting." He hung up.

Most interesting? thought Henry. Could it be as simple as that, then? Had Casewait surprised some common car thieves in the middle of the night and somehow gotten himself shot? But then he would have had to clean up the house, take a nap, and then blunder out of the house at seven twenty in the morning to take a swim. Not impossible. Henry had heard amazing stories of people walking around with bullets in them, some of them even unaware they had been shot. And the unknown visitor in the car who had departed so suddenly? It *could* have been no more than a stranger asking directions—people were always losing themselves in the area—a stranger who may have come upon Casewait staggering around with a bullet in him and decided to clear out as fast as possible. A stranger who may have had reasons for not coming forward.

Henry began to feel much better. Morris was probably right; this could be the simplest sort of case. At any minute some conscience-stricken stranger might come forward and clear the whole thing up, and incidentally get Henry off the hook he still felt he was impaled on.

Henry now felt really splendid and looked forward to a few hours well spent working. He had just begun to make his preparations for the trip to his little shed when he was caught up by a truly appalling thought that brought his buoyant mood crashing to earth.

"Go into the city?" he said to himself.

9

Henry stood on the southbound platform of the suburban railroad station awaiting the 8:36 local-express to the city. His mood was sour and his outlook dark, despite the clear and sunny day. He had chosen this train because it was the last one before the end of the rush hour, when all express service stopped and the succeeding trains seemed to inch their way into the city. Also, the cars of the 8:36 were usually free of the shoppers and matinee-goers who refused to follow the rigid decorum of the commuters, who over the years had worked out a code of conduct that allowed them to arrive at their destination still reasonably sane. The first and most important rule in this code was that there should be no unnecessary conversation except among the bridge players, who paid for this privilege by earning the undying enmity of their fellow passengers. Obviously, women dressed to the nines, wearing gloves, and carrying smart shopping bags could hardly be expected to accede to this rule, which was why their husbands forbade them under pain of death or separation, whichever they deemed worse, to ride the 8:36 or any earlier train.

Henry surveyed his fellow passengers, a mixed lot of what could be called media or communications people—publishers, advertising men, broadcasters, and various people somehow connected with the arts. The stockbrokers, bankers, shop owners, and various others who had to be at their desks by the time the nation's money began changing hands had long since departed on the earlier trains. The 8:36 people, however, did not have to appear in the presence of their minions or masters until ten o'clock at the earliest. Indeed, they would suffer severe loss of status if they ever did happen to wander into their offices before the coffee break. Most of them were familiar to Henry, who nodded now and again to an acquaintance. They did not ask him where he had been or what he was doing, however, probably assuming that he had taken an earlier train for a while or had just suffered the periodic unemployment that regularly thinned their ranks.

Henry noted with approval a slight change that had taken place since his last trip to the city: to judge from the attire of his platform companions, the great international costume party had begun to wind down. Although its outward form had changed from year to year or season to season, this phenomenon had remained remarkably constant since its beginnings in the late sixties, when people first began to think it imperative that they make a statement about themselves with their clothes. Henry felt that if all these separate statements had been summed up in one grand statement, it would be "I'm adorable."

The last year in which Henry had commuted fairly regularly, the prevailing style had seemed to be a mixture of the combat attire of the two world wars. He well remembered an advertising executive who affected a wool olive drab GI overcoat of the Siege of Bastogne era, the type that reached nearly to the ankles and was usually worn with mud-encrusted galoshes. The adman accented this ensemble with an attaché case that was really a schoolchild's lunch pail decorated with decals of popular comic strip characters. He was reputed to be a genius in direct mail.

On Henry's rare recent trips the prevailing mode had seemed to be that of a working ranch, dominated by faded jeans and short denim jackets with cuffs turned up at the wrists. But since then a more conservative note seemed to have been struck, perhaps reflecting the political mood of the country, and it looked to Henry as if these weathervanes of popular trends assembled around him were returning to the basics. When he had last seen the elderly woman standing next to him, whom he knew to be a powerful fashion editor of a women's magazine, she had looked as though she were headed for a gunfight at the O.K. Corral. But now, dressed in a plaid skirt with a blue blazer, she might have been just down from Smith or Holyoke and taking the train into the city to meet her mother for lunch at the Colony Club.

Henry and a few others in the rapidly increasing platform crowd wore traditional city garb, of course, and there were certain holdovers from earlier waves of style who were either slow on the uptake or too financially strapped to make any contemporary statements about themselves. Henry noticed a few Edwardian dandies and one large black man who was dressed like Allan Quartermain as played by Stewart Granger in *King Solomon's Mines*. There were a few other variations on the still popular white-hunter style, but the black carried it off with much more panache. Henry would have unhesitatingly put him in charge of the impromptu safari that could have been assembled right there on the platform of the small suburban station.

As the train jolted and lurched toward the city, Henry sat next to the window on the river side of the car and stared gloomily at the parking lots and small local stations passing by. He had never been able to sleep on the train, which had made commuting doubly painful for him. What a gift, he thought, as he glanced at the middle-aged wrangler dozing beside him, to be able to board one of these scandalously inefficient and filthy cars and slip into oblivion, to be awakened at the other end, depressingly in the city or joyously at your home station.

The car was crowded and there were several standees, including the black Allan Quartermain, who gazed morosely at the advertisements or at the moisture condensing on the ceiling and dripping on unwary heads. The rest of the cowpunchers, gunslingers, fops, grizzled veterans of two wars, white hunters, and squares—in which category Henry gladly included himself—read the *Times*, dozed, or conversed within the bounds of propriety. Mercifully there were no bridge players to enrage them with their sudden outbursts of analysis after each hand. Outside the filthy windows the suburbs began to give way to the industrial wastelands of the inner suburbs. Henry thought of the old newspaper joke:

> Managing editor to reporter: "In this suicide story you say the woman threw herself into the melancholy waters of the Hudson River. Now, will you tell me just what the hell makes the Hudson so melancholy."
> Reporter to managing editor: (Pause) "It has to pass by Yonkers?"

It is said that great civilizations flourish only along the banks of great rivers, but it seemed to Henry that something had obviously gone wrong here. His depression deepened the closer they drew to "the Rock," as the city was known among commuters. It was a rock from which Henry had escaped as gratefully as any inmate of Alcatraz or Devil's Island, and he dreaded ever going back. He feared that those impenetrable walls would close around him once again, dooming him to an endless round of editorial meetings, huge lunches, and pointless parties from which he would be delivered only by the Great Executioner himself in the form of a drug-crazed mugger or some overzealous cop with poor marksmanship—that was, if the poisonous air and the murderous traffic didn't get him first.

After a truly disheartening delay in the tunnel, the train somehow made it down the hill and onto the lower-level tracks. If it could be said of a train that it staggered, this train staggered up to its platform and expired with an exhausted hiss from its brakes. The passengers fled the cars as from the scene of an accident, managing as best they could in their high-heeled boots, painfully tight Italian shoes, and heavy paratrooper footgear. Henry somehow gained the platform and started morosely up the long ramp that he had always thought would make a good setting for a scene in an expressionist film. He was spewed along with the crowd into the brightly lit lower level and was carried by the human swarm toward the stairs to the main concourse. From there he hurried to the west-side entrance and gained the top before turning to witness the scene below. From this vantage he could say with Shakespeare's melancholy Jacques addressing the heedless deer, "Press on, you fat and greasy citizens!" He fled the building and entered the great city.

Henry stood in front of the narrow building in the West Forties, his worst suspicions confirmed. The building was squeezed between an art supply store on one side and a discount drugstore on the other. The entrance was one step down from the sidewalk and consisted of a small foyer and blank door with a peephole probably left over from Prohibition days, to judge by the age and condition of the whole area. In the foyer there was a directory of sorts, listing a few employment agencies, a costume jewelry importer, and several names with no indication of business. CASEWAIT ENTERPRISES, 6TH FL. therefore seemed a touch of class in this motley of cheap detachable lettering. Several handprinted index cards promoting various jobs, mostly stenographic, were stuck at random around the directory—probably the employment agencies' only form of advertising. Henry examined a few and found them so dubious that he was shocked in spite of himself.

He was reminded of London after the Street Acts, when the jolly streetwalkers of Piccadilly Circus and Leicester Square were forced indoors and had to keep in touch with their clientele through just such notices posted in shop windows and convenient public places.

Henry had tried calling the managers of the building, a certain Klein and his associates, whose name and number he had found among Casewait's papers, but had not been able to make a connection. The phone had been temporarily disconnected, a recorded voice had told him. That, Henry knew, could mean just about anything. Perfectly respectable businesses had their phones temporarily disconnected all the time through no fault of their own. He had heard a story, probably spurious, that even Merrill Lynch had had their phones temporarily disconnected, causing havoc in the market. Everyone thought they couldn't pay their phone bill.

Rather than track Klein Associates to their lair downtown, Henry had decided to go directly to Casewait's office and inspect it briefly before proceeding further. He entered the narrow lobby, which was surprisingly clean and well kept, and pushed the button for the elevator, a self-operated affair that clanged open immediately. He stepped into the bare cubicle and had a mild coronary seizure as the car dropped about six inches and then slowly regained the level of the lobby. Henry considered the wisdom of going any further, but then, against all reason, pushed the button for the sixth floor. The door clanged shut and Henry had some inkling of what it must be like for an astronaut after he has been sealed in his capsule. With a great banging and whirring the elevator blasted off and after a mercifully slow ascent arrived at the sixth floor, where it bobbed uncertainly for an eternity and then came to rest. The door opened and Henry leapt gratefully into a bare hallway, which, like the lobby, was clean and free of the usual assaults on the senses one meets in such places. If nothing else, the building had a good janitor, thought Henry as he cased the area.

Casewait Enterprises shared the sixth floor with the Ace Employment Agency, which occupied the front half of the building. Henry thought of paying a courtesy call on Ace to let them know that he was entering the neighboring office legally, but he had the distinct feeling that he would be disturbing someone's midmorning nap. The Ace Employment Agency was not thriving, to judge by the deathly silence emanating from behind the closed door.

Henry went to the door of Casewait Enterprises, which was identified by one of those plastic nameplates that could be purchased and inscribed at any locksmith's and then stuck to a door. He tried the knob, but the door was locked. He took out the key ring that the police had given to him along with Casewait's other personal effects; he found the right key almost at once, and let himself into the office. Behind him he heard the elevator clatter and whine as it descended.

The office consisted of two rooms, the first of which must have served as a reception area, since it contained a cracked leather sofa, a straight-backed chair with a badly worn upholstered seat, and a scarred coffee table. The floor was covered with speckled linoleum designed not to show the dirt. The second room was directly behind the first, separated from it by a frosted-glass partition; there was no door between the two rooms, just a gap in the partition. The second room contained a desk, a chair, and a file cabinet; the walls were bare. There was a desk calculator on a movable stand next to the desk, but no typewriter. The desk held only a telephone and a desk calendar–appointment pad, opened, Henry noticed, to the day before Casewait's death. There were no drapes or blinds on the windows, which looked onto the uncompromisingly ugly rears of the buildings on the next block. Henry hoped that Casewait had done his consulting in expensive restaurants rather than here.

The only unusual feature in the room was a small safe in the corner of the room behind the desk. It was not the heavy, dark, old-fashioned type on casters that Henry associated with small, marginal businesses; this was a gleaming modern job with Yale locks as well as a combination, and looked fiendishly difficult to open, even if you knew how. Fortunately the safe was wide open and, not so fortunately, completely empty. No ledgers, no contracts, no bills, no receipts—nothing. Henry turned to the file cabinet and opened it drawer by drawer. Nothing. The desk drawers were also empty, except for some legal pads and pencils and a phone book. Casewait had not even had stationery with his letterhead on it. The whole place was devoid of any sign of the business that was supposed to have been carried on there. Henry lifted the receiver of the desk phone and heard a dial tone. Well, he thought, at least one thing was used. That, and the safe, obviously.

Henry sat down in the desk chair and pondered the situation. Deep within the building the elevator clanged and whirred as another reckless soul decided to take his or her chances. Henry had come to the inescapable conclusion that Casewait Enterprises was not an ongoing business. So just what was it? A front for something? That was perfectly in keeping with Casewait's moral and ethical code—but at least you'd expect to find a postage stamp in the place. Or was he wrong? Had Casewait Enterprises simply been cleaned out by thieves? No; the only valuable thing in the place besides the safe was the calculator, which was highly fenceable as well as portable, and that had not been taken.

Henry consulted his notebook and then picked up the phone and dialed Klein Associates. A recorded voice again told him that the number was temporarily out of order. Henry replaced the receiver and pondered calling the police, but he didn't think he could bear to go through the preliminaries that such an action would involve. Compared with the city's police, his township's were reckless in their haste to come to one's assistance. He decided to seek out the building's efficient janitor and ask some questions himself for a change.

He gave the office another cursory glance and then left. In the hall, he turned to reinsert the key and lock the door and suddenly felt a curious pressure on the back of his head. Instantaneously a hundred flashbulbs went off behind his eyes and he fell against the door, pushing it open as he crashed to the floor. His head seemed to be expanding at about the same rate as the universe, and then just as rapidly contracting until it became a black hole. He had rolled over onto his back, and just before blacking out completely, he saw, as though through the end of a long tunnel or the rifled barrel of a cannon, the silhouette of his attacker. He was wearing a white-hunter's hat like the one worn by Allan Quartermain as played by Stewart Granger in *King Solomon's Mines*, costarring Deborah Kerr. . . .

10

HENRY OPENED HIS eyes and said, "Hello," to the young man bending over him. "How are you?" He was in a friendly mood, and the young man seemed pleasant and good at his work, which seemed to consist of shining lights in people's eyes.

"How do you feel?" said the young man, dropping Henry's eyelid and snapping off his pencil flashlight.

"Just fine," said Henry. He seemed to be lying on his back. "Now if I could just get up off this floor . . ." He attempted to raise his head and was regaled with a colored light show behind his eyeballs.

"Not so fast," said the young man, restraining him by pressing the palm of his hand against Henry's chest. "Do you know where you are?" he asked.

Hmm, thought Henry. It started to come back. "I think I'm in the offices, or office, of Casewait Enterprises. Right?" he asked.

"Yep," said the young man. "Now raise your head slowly and try to sit up." He assisted Henry by putting one hand under his shoulders and lifting slightly, encouragingly.

Henry raised his head, was treated to another engaging light show behind his eyeballs, and then slowly sat up. He noticed that there was another pleasant young man in the room, dressed in white, as was the one who was helping to steady himself. An older man, clad in something dark, was sitting above him and to one side. "Who are you?" said Henry to the room at large.

"He looks okay," said the one pleasant young man to the other. "What do you think?"

"Look at my finger," said the other, kneeling in front of Henry, who was smiling at them both. The young man moved his raised finger slowly across Henry's line of vision, and Henry followed it with his eyes. "Can you feel this?" said the young man, squeezing Henry's left hand. Henry nodded. "And this?" squeezing the right. Henry nodded again. The young man looked questioningly at his companion.

"I don't know," said the other, who then went around behind Henry and knelt down. "Let's have a look at his head," he said, and began gingerly probing at Henry's pate. "The skin's not broken," he said. Henry smiled happily.

"Man," said the young man, "you sure got yourself sapped.

Henry nodded agreeably.

"Sandbagged," said the other young man.

The smile was beginning to fade from Henry's face. "Coshed?" he asked.

"Are you British, Mr, ah, Wilnot?" said the dark-clad man, consulting something in his hand.

"Will-nut," said Henry, taking in the man in more detail.

"What?"

"It's pronounced Will-nut, my name," said Henry, noticing that what the man was holding was his wallet.

"Well, Mr. Wilnot, are you British?"

"No," said Henry, "I just read a great many British mystery novels."

"I see," said the dark man, to whom it seemed a perfectly reasonable answer.

Henry became acutely aware of a throbbing sensation at the back of his head. He moved his hand to feel it and the pleasant young man grabbed it and said "Don't touch! We'll put something on it for you." The other young man moved in back of Henry and sprayed something from an aerosol can on his head. Henry felt instantly better.

"I don't think there's any concussion," said the young man. "He was just in wonderland for a while. We could take him over to Roosevelt or Bellevue for a check-up."

Bellevue! thought Henry, alarmed. Scenes from an old Ray Milland movie flashed through his mind.

"No, no," said the dark man. "If you don't think it's necessary there's no need to take the trouble. Can he get up?"

"Sure," said the young man, and he and his companion helped Henry to his feet and sat him in the straight-backed chair next to the desk. "You okay?"

"Yes," said Henry. "Could I try standing up?"

"Sure. Why not?" After conducting several experiments in balance and coordination on him, the two paramedics or ambulance attendants, or even ambulance *drivers* for all Henry knew, pronounced him reasonably fit. "You better check with your own doctor when you get home," said one.

Henry nodded. He noticed that a uniformed policeman stood outside the door to the outer office and that a few people were gawking past him at Henry. The two white-clad young men departed.

"Who are you?" asked Henry of the dark man.

"Sergeant Gianinni, Twenty-sixth Precinct," he said, flashing some credential that Henry did not have a chance to look at. "I should tell you that normally a uniformed officer would take care of this, but I'm part of a special squad that has been set up to investigate any muggings in this area."

I am honored, thought Henry.

"The mayor is doing everything he can to cut down on street violence and has assigned the top men in the department to the job," Gianinni said with a self-satisfied smile.

"I would vote for the man if I could," said Henry.

"Yes," said Gianinni. "I see that you're from out of town. Now, Mr. Wilnot," he said briskly, getting down to business, "can you tell me just what happened?"

Henry told him quickly why he was in the office of Casewait Enterprises. "I believe that that's my wallet you have there, and you must have noticed that there is a letter testamentary tucked in it, which explains my right to enter these premises."

Gianinni nodded and obligingly unfolded the letter and affected to read it carefully, as if he had not already done so.

"I was leaving the office and had turned to lock the door," continued Henry, "when I was struck from behind."

"Did you see who it was who struck you?"

"Just before blacking out I'm pretty sure I glimpsed a tall, heavily built black man who dressed like . . . I mean, he was wearing a khaki safari suit—you know, the kind with a hip-length jacket with short sleeves and a belt in the back—and a wide-brimmed . . . ah, hat . . . the kind that people who shoot tigers and elephants wear."

"A white-hunter's hat," said Gianinni helpfully.

"Exactly," said Henry.

Gianinni noted all of this in a notebook. "Now, Mr. Wilnot, will you look through your wallet and tell me if anything is missing. We had to remove it from you to find out who you were, by the way."

"Of course," said Henry. He took his wallet and examined it. Thirty-three dollars, credit cards, driver's license, odds and ends, pictures of his ungrateful and rebellious children; nothing seemed to be missing.

"Will you look through your pockets please?" said Gianinni.

Henry understood an order when he heard one. He stood and emptied his pockets onto the desktop. Loose change, his train ticket receipt, pocket comb, handkerchief, some stubs from the last time he and Erica had gone to the movies . . .

"Wait a minute," said Henry, slapping the inside pockets of his suit jacket. "I seem to be missing . . . Yes, my keys, they're gone!"

"That's all?" said Gianinni. "Nothing else is missing?"

"No," said Henry, "that's all, I'm pretty sure." He was still patting all of his pockets.

"What kind of keys? Were they on a chain?"

"They were on a ring," said Henry. "My car keys—two,

one for the ignition and one for the trunk—and house keys, of course, and a key to a strongbox I bought years ago and never use. I keep meaning to take it off the ring but never get around to it."

"Were they these?" asked Gianinni, holding up a key ring.

Henry examined them and said, "No, these are the keys I let myself in with. They're part of the estate mentioned in the letter testamentary." They were just ordinary keys; car, house, miscellaneous, the same as Henry's. "I wonder why he didn't take these? Where did you find them?"

"In the door," said Gianinni uninterestedly. He seemed preoccupied with his notes. "And now, Mr. Wilnot . . . " He looked at Henry levelly.

Oh, oh, thought Henry, here comes something.

"Did you take anything from this office, something that is no longer in your possession?"

Henry was startled by the question. "No, no!" he said, perhaps a little too vehemently.

"You're sure of that?" said Gianinni suspiciously.

"Absolutely sure," said Henry, looking as sincere as possible.

Gianinni gave him a sour look and continued, "Do you know any reason why anyone would attack you for the purpose of stealing your keys?"

"God knows," said Henry desperately. "Anyone who would steal my car would have to be crazy. And my house—there's always someone there and no one would want to break in. And besides—" He caught himself.

"It's being watched," Gianinni finished for him. "Or at least, the house next door is. You're involved in a murder investigation, aren't you, Mr. Wilnot?"

"Yes," said Henry. He didn't have to ask how Gianinni knew; there must be all-points bulletins out on Casewait's car, the car in front of the house, the weapon, and God knows what else those seemingly ineffectual men in the mobile crime lab must have found or deduced.

"I'd better tell you something, Sergeant," said Henry. He then told Gianinni all about seeing the black white hunter on the station platform and on the train. "I believe now that I was followed into the city. I would have told you about this before, but the, how shall I put it? The *flow* of our conversation didn't give me the opportunity."

"I see," said Gianinni noncommittally, making more notes in his little book. "Well," he said, "that should about do it, Mr. Wilnot. Do you feel well enough to make it home by yourself, or would you like me to make some arrangements for you?"

You might call back those two ambulance drivers to give me another shot of that stuff on the back of my head, Henry thought. In addition to the throbbing, which had returned twice as strong, he had a spectacular headache. "No, I'll make it all right," he said aloud. "My car's at the station."

"But you don't have any keys."

Get off my back about keys, thought Henry. "I'll call my wife," he said and rose unsteadily to pocket his belongings from the top of the desk. "Who found me, by the way?" he asked.

"Somebody who was looking for the employment agency at the other end of the hall."

"Did she get the job?" said Henry irrelevantly.

"How did you know it was a woman?" said Gianinni.

"Don't you guys ever give up?" said Henry. "I'm going home."

Henry bought a bottle of aspirin and a can of club soda at the station and medicated himself all the way home. Even so, the train ride was excruciatingly painful. It was still early afternoon when he boarded the train and congratulated himself upon finding an almost empty car in which he could put his feet up on the seat facing his and attain as near a horizontal position as possible, which somewhat eased his pain. But just moments before the train pulled out, a gang of mothers and raucous children charged into the car and took over almost all of the available seats, including the ones across from Henry's. They had all just come from a circus or a matinee or some other entertainment that must have encouraged them to scream throughout the performance. Thus primed, they took advantage of the train ride to dissipate the vocal energy they had built up over the past few hours. Henry could only console himself with Walt Whitman's "I am the man, I suffer'd, I was there."

The train was a local, and the screaming children and shrieking women began dropping behind in small groups until, somewhere in the outer suburbs, a great squawking mob of them fell away and the car was left in relative peace.

In his pain, Henry reviewed his interview with Sergeant Gianinni. He was bothered by the feeling that there was something that had been left unsaid, some half-formed thought that was not expressed or had been cut off before it had been completed. He was sure that it had something to do with his keys. He went over the exchange with Gianinni: the policeman asked why anyone would want to steal his keys and he had said no one would want to steal his car, et cetera, et cetera. Then somehow Gianinni had interrupted him and sprung that business of his being involved in a murder investigation. Then Henry had said that no one would want to break into his house because—no, no, *that* was when Gianinni had broken in to say because it was being watched. What else had he, Henry, been going to say at that point? Something about the other key on his key chain, the key to his strongbox. He was going to say that no one would want to break into his strongbox because it was empty. But there was something else about that key . . . Of course! It was completely different from the other keys on the ring. It was much smaller and very thin, just like one of those keys they use for mailboxes in apartment houses, or just like the key— That was it! he thought triumphantly.

Just like the key he had found in the lock of Casewait's swimming-pool filtering system.

11

THE NEXT MORNING, after returning from his doctor's, where he had been pronounced free of concussion, Henry retired to his study and contemplated the key he had found at the lock of Casewait's pool filtering system. There was no doubt about it: it was either a key to a mailbox, an attaché case, a strongbox, or something else in which one would keep papers or small valuables. Did Casewait have a second set of books stashed somewhere? That might explain the secrecy, though Henry of all people should recognize the "Purloined Letter" gambit when he saw it, which dictated that the best place to hide something was the most obvious: ergo, the safest place to hide a key was in a lock.

There was something more important about this key, however, something Henry had determined only after long thought and ruling out every other possibility: it must have been what Casewait was seeking when he had staggered, seriously wounded, out his back door that morning four days ago. Henry also had the curious feeling that this was what Casewait had charged him with in his rather odd letter.

Henry looked at the stacks of Loeb's Classics sitting on his desk. Jeanette had presented them to him, not knowing, of course, that Casewait had willed them to Henry—and Henry had no intention of telling her that he had—along with some framed prints from Casewait's study that Henry had admired in the past. These then were his payment—but for what?

Henry picked up one of the volumes. Martial. He thumbed through it, looking for something familiar. Like most people, he could translate only those passages he had memorized as a schoolboy, and Martial had not exactly been recommended to Henry and his horny little classmates. He replaced the Martial and looked for something a bit more conventional. The *Eclogues* were always reassuring; one didn't forget *everything*. He opened the book to the familiar first lines: *Tityre, tu patulae recubans sub tegmine fagi* . . . Sounds as though it should be the state motto of California, thought Henry. The best modern translation of *recubans* would *have* to be "laid back."

California reminded Henry of his son, Harold, who was attending Berkeley in pursuit of some degree in one of the social disciplines, as they were called with a straight face by their practitioners. Henry had last heard from him more than a month ago when Harold had called—collect, of course—to ask Henry to sell his amplifiers and other electronic gear left over from his rock-star phase and send him the money as soon as possible.

"What's the matter?" Henry had asked. "Do you need the money for grass or dynamite?"

"Oh, for Christ's sake, Dad, that's all over; it has been for some time. Can I talk to Mom?"

"Yes, but try to keep your speech at least acceptable to our prim eastern ears."

"Oh, for God's sake," said Harold. "Berkeley's not like that anymore, and probably never was anyway."

"Look, son," Henry had said, "whether you like it or not, that diploma mill in which you've chosen to spend your declining years is fixed in the public mind with obscenity as indelibly as Worcestershire is with steak sauce." He paused to consider the sentence for a moment. Could it be improved? the artist in him asked. He thought not.

Henry put away the Virgil and located Suetonius. Even Latinists would opt for trash when given the choice, he thought, and settled down to bring himself up to date on the goings-on at Tiberius's Caprian villa. Jeanette suddenly appeared at the doorway and asked if she could come in. "Of course," said Henry. "Make yourself comfortable. I've just been admiring my new acquisitions."

"Yes, they are nice, aren't they," she said, "and I'm so glad you can use them. I always thought it was a great waste to have them just sitting there."

Henry, who hardly spent time reading Latin poetry, didn't quite know what to say, but managed "Well, at least they never got damaged."

"Yes," she said nervously. She squeezed one hand in the other and bit her lower lip. Either she was genuinely disturbed, thought Henry, or was giving a very good imitation of a rattled woman. "Henry, I've got to talk to you about this . . . this whatever's happening. I feel terrible about your getting mixed up in all of it."

"Well, don't," said Henry. "Besides, it was Joe who appointed me executor—or coexecutor."

"I just wish you'd turn the whole thing over to a lawyer or to the bank. I don't want something worse happening to you."

"What do you mean?"

"Look, Henry, don't pretend that what happened to you yesterday was just one of those things that happen to you in the city. You could have been killed!"

"Oh, really, Jeanette, it wasn't that bad," Henry said.

Jeanette fingered her pearl necklace and stared out of the window for a while, then said, "Henry, I haven't told anyone of this, but I think Joe was mixed up in something crooked. I mean something *really* crooked."

"Oh," said Henry. "With whom?"

"I don't know. But he used to get these strange phone calls. He never let me answer the phone while he was there, but one night he was out and I answered one of the calls, and the man on the other end sounded suspicious."

"What did he say?"

"Oh, he didn't *say* anything suspicious, he just sounded

suspicious. I mean he didn't sound like anyone Joe should know through his business. I thought for a while that Joe might be gambling or had run in to debt, but I decided that wasn't it because he kept talking about making it big at last. And the last time I spoke to him he said something about leaving the country or moving somewhere we—he could start over again."

"When was this?" asked Henry. "I didn't know you had talked to him recently."

"Oh, I don't know; three, four weeks ago," she said. "You know, Henry, he wanted me to come back to him."

"No, I didn't know that," said Henry. "And what did you say to that, if you don't mind my asking."

"Oh, Henry, really! What could I say? You know as well as I that I could never go—have gone back to him. And besides," she said, suddenly shy, "I've met someone else. Erica may have mentioned it."

"Yes, she did," said Henry. "She's very happy for you, and so am I. You deserve something good after what you've been through. Who is he? Anyone I would know?

"He's the head of my agency; I don't think you would have heard of him. Anyway, he's something new to me—on a personal, intimate level, that is—a genuinely good and kind man who seems to think of me more than himself. He was divorced a few years ago, his children are all grown, and I believe he is looking for a friend as well as companion or partner or whatever you want to call it. It would have been impossible to go back to Joe after meeting Barney, no matter how much he claimed to have changed."

"Joe had changed?" said Henry. "He didn't seem that way to me!"

"Well, he claimed he had, and that he wanted to make it all up to me and start over somewhere else." She paused a moment, and then she said rather timidly, "You know, this—what has happened—makes it much easier for me. I think he may have given me trouble over a divorce."

"He probably would have," said Henry, nodding. "The idea for a divorce would have had to come from him, probably, or not at all."

"I'm positive you're right," said Jeanette, relieved. "I know he would have made life hell for me." She thought awhile more. "But what I really want now is for you not to get mixed up in Joe's affairs, whatever they were. I just have a feeling that they were dishonest and, well, dangerous."

"Have you told Detective Lieutenant Morris this?" asked Henry. "He'd like to know, I'm sure."

"No," she said. "For some reason at the time I thought I'd shield Joe from any more shame. But then this thing happened to you and I realized I made a mistake, that I should have told the police of my suspicions."

"Well, I don't think it would have mattered much. He probably would have taken it with a grain of salt, and I doubt if it would have deterred me."

"There, now," she said, getting up from the ottoman where she had been perched. "I feel much better about things. Just promise me that you won't go off on your own again. I'll tell that nice detective all about Joe's calls when he comes over here this afternoon. What do you think he wants, by the way?"

"Probably just to get us to tell our stories again, just in case we forgot something the first time, as you did, or to see if we change them in any way. I think we can expect a lot more of that before the case is closed."

"I'm positive," Jeanette said firmly, "that Joe's . . . strange activities are behind all of this, and especially behind his being killed."

"I hope you're right," said Henry, getting up from his chair and replacing the Suetonius. "At least it takes the suspicion from me."

"Oh, Henry, you can't be serious!"

"Think it over. So far I'm the only one who had the chance, or even has a motive, such as it is."

"A motive! Henry what possible motive could you have had for killing Joe?"

"I admit it isn't much, but the police are liable to latch on to anything if they're stumped."

"But what *is* your motive?"

"Extreme irritation," said Henry. He was not joking. Casewait had more than once moved him to a quiet fury with his unstated contempt for his work. Whether it was Casewait's refusal to admit that he had ever read one of the copies of his books Henry had regularly presented to him during the early days of their friendship, or the offhand way he would stroll unannounced into Henry's shed while Henry was in the throes of composition and casually pick up a page from the stack of manuscript at the side of the desk, read it silently, nodding his head as if in confirmation of a preconceived notion, and then replace it on the stack and walk quietly out the door, Henry was convinced it was devised to enrage him. And it succeeded marvelously.

The genres in which Henry worked required—indeed, demanded—at least three sex scenes per book, each one more highly charged than the last. Early on, Henry had devised his own formula for these obligatory passages and they soon became routine—there are, after all, only so many orifices and not that many positions—so he had turned to description. Unfortunately, like so many of his contemporaries, he had been influenced by the movie *Tom Jones*, specifically by the supper scene and all it had to say about the eroticism of food and eating. No matter how he fought it, Henry's private eyes and undercover agents, even his cowboys, had women with thighs as white and smooth as cream cheese, nipples as pink as the finest smoked salmon, lips like strawberries, eyes as black as ripe olives, and so on and on. One day Casewait strolled into his shed just as Henry had finished a page of such description and picked it up and read it silently. He carefully replaced the page of manuscript on its pile and said, "Sounds like a deli," and walked out the door. Henry had been so upset that he had not been able to write another word all morning, and had spent the afternoon unblocking with his bottle of vodka. Some time later he learned that Casewait was referring to him behind his back as the master of the take-out school of erotic literature.

Jeanette laughed. "You're just joking, aren't you?"

"No, I'm not. Listen, just a few months ago a mass murderer tried to justify what he'd done by saying that the barking of his neighbor's dog was driving him crazy. The police have even started taking complaints about noisy parties seriously. They show up with riot guns and surround the house."

"God," said Jeanette, amused, "and you people talk about California!"

"Anyway, who else have they got? All the evidence that Joe was killed by someone else depends on me. Even the exact time of the murder depends on me, and I think they'd feel much better if it had happened in the middle of the night sometime."

"But wouldn't that tend to prove your innocence? Why would you make up a story like that. You could just as well have told them what they wanted to hear."

"Yes, and then I really would have been in trouble."

Detective Lieutenant Morris received Jeanette's new information with equanimity. "I see," he said, making some notations in his ever ready notebook. "Very interesting." He had brought someone with him whom he introduced as his associate, a Detective Harrison, who also made notes in his little book. Perhaps recording his arrival and introduction, thought Henry.

They had all—Henry, Erica, Jeanette, Jane—told their stories anew for the benefit of Detective Harrison, a dark, heavyset man who listened to them all impassively. Henry found him eminently satisfactory as a detective.

"Now, then, here's how it stands," said Detective

Lieutenant Morris. "At seven twenty in the morning Mr. Wilnot observed Mr. Casewait emerging from his back door and staggering or stumbling in the direction of his backyard swimming pool. At the same time, Mr. Wilnot heard a car start and depart at some speed from the area in the front and to the side of Mr. Casewait's house. At approximately seven twenty-five Mr. Wilnot observed Mr. Casewait floating in his swimming pool and dashed through the, ah, dividing shrubbery"—Henry winced—"and fished, I mean, retrieved the body of Mr. Casewait from the pool and determined that he was dead.

"At approximately seven thirty you, Mrs. Wilnot, were awakened by your husband, who informed you that Mr. Casewait had been shot and that he, your husband, was calling the police. Our log at the station shows that we received a call at exactly seven thirty-five from Mr. Wilnot asking for assistance. Doesn't that seem like rather a long time to place an emergency call, Mr. Wilnot, five minutes?"

"It seemed more like fifteen," said Henry.

Lieutenant Morris chose to overlook the remark. "At seven fifty, Sergeant Greaves and two uniformed officers arrived on the scene and were followed shortly by the sheriff and a detective.

"Now nothing else of any particular interest to us here happened until five thirty P.M., when Officer Bierson contacted Mrs. Casewait at her home in Los Angeles. Now let's see, that's in Inglewood, isn't it, Mrs. Casewait?"

"Yes, Marina del Rey," said Jeanette. Apparently this meant something to both of them, but to Henry it was merely another of the myriad towns of Los Angeles County, the status of which, except for Beverly Hills, he knew nothing about.

"Officer Bierson had begun calling your residence and office; those addresses and/or numbers had been supplied to us by Mrs. Wilnot"—he bowed graciously to Erica, who just as graciously accepted his thanks—"at one o'clock, after he had finished his duties at the Casewait house and returned to the station. Officer Bierson was assigned this task by Sergeant Greaves, since all other officers and detectives were occupied." Was this Morris's way of apologizing for Bierson's telephone style, wondered Henry, or was he getting at something else?

"Officer Bierson," Morris continued, "first called your office, since it would be ten o'clock California time, and was told that you were not there and had not been since the day before the previous day."

"That's right," said Jeanette. "I had been checking on some clients who were working, and I was visiting some kennels and stables in the area. I handle many animal clients," she explained. Morris and Harrison didn't seem particularly interested.

"Could you tell us, Mrs. Casewait," said Morris, "where you were the previous night?"

Jeanette looked startled and annoyed. "Why, yes," she said. "I was having dinner with my—with a friend. A Mr. Barney Thomas, who is the president and chief executive officer of the talent agency I work for. I believe you have the number."

"Yes, thank you," said Morris, looking at Harrison, who made a note in his little book. "Now, can you tell us at what time you arrived home on the night that Officer Bierson called to tell you of the death of your husband?"

"Well, it was hardly the night. I believe it was about two thirty in the afternoon when I received his call. I had returned home a short time before, maybe half an hour."

"Wouldn't it be normal for you to have returned to your office that early in the afternoon, after your business calls, that is?"

"Yes, except my apartment is along the route back to my office from the Valley—I had been looking at some kennels up there—and I thought I would stop by and freshen up. We're in the middle of a heat wave and drought. I had planned to make some phone calls from home after calling my office. Your man called before I could get started."

"And then you immediately called Mrs. Wilnot here, is that correct?"

"Yes. It was about two forty-five then, I'm sure. Anyway, you can check my phone bill."

"There's no need for that, Mrs. Casewait," said Morris. "We are just trying to establish the sequence and exact time of everything that happened that day. We either do it now or we will have to bother you for corroboration after you have returned to California."

"I see," said Jeanette. "Of course. I understand. I'm sorry if I seem irritated, but I don't see—"

"As Mr. Wilnot will tell you," said Morris, nodding deferentially to the distinguished mystery writer Henry Wilnot, "this is a standard procedure which never, *never* fails to achieve at least some result, no matter how small."

Jeanette subsided into silence.

"You then caught the three fifteen flight to the city, arriving at eleven twenty, our time," continued Morris. "You rented a car and drove here to Mr. and Mrs. Wilnot's house, arriving at approximately twelve thirty, is that correct?"

"Yes," said Jeanette grudgingly, and Henry and Erica nodded in agreement.

"At twelve forty you placed an overseas call to the Hotel du Plessis and attempted to contact your stepdaughter, Jane."

"Well, actually, it was a group effort," said Jeanette. "I believe Henry placed the call and Erica took it from there."

"Ah, yes," said Morris. "You gave them the number and they placed the call and received the information."

"Yes," said Jeanette, rather testily, Henry thought.

"And you—or, rather, Mrs. Wilnot was told that Miss Casewait had not yet checked in, although she had a reservation for the evening of the day before. It was then seven forty-five in Paris."

Since no one offered any objections to his analysis, Morris then turned to Jane, who was sitting unobtrusively in a corner chair, her hands folded in her lap and her ankles crossed, an odd pose for an adult woman but one Henry recognized as entirely defensive, carefully designed to conceal or at least disguise her limbs. As always, when he saw her thus disposed, a heaviness settled on Henry's heart.

"Why weren't you there, Miss Casewait?" asked Morris.

Jane looked up and gazed at him serenely. "I was on the way to my hotel from Charles de Gaulle Airport," she said, "which is quite a distance from Paris. The flight I had taken from Lyon was delayed when they had to make an unscheduled stop at Dijon to accommodate some important businessman."

"I thought you had come from Lausanne," said Morris.

"I had. Some of our people were taking the Society's minibus to Lyon for reassignment, and I thought I'd catch a ride with them and take a flight from there. It's a very nice trip."

"When did you finally arrive in Paris?"

"Not until about three thirty or so in the afternoon. I went straight to the hotel and found the message from Mrs. Wilnot waiting for me."

Morris seemed to ponder this for a moment, and then said unexpectedly, "Could I see your passport, please?"

"Why, yes," said Jane, not at all disturbed. "I'll get it for you." She left the room.

"What's this all about, Lieutenant?"asked Henry. "Surely you don't think—"

"Please, Mr. Wilnot, I explained all of this to you just the other day. We check *everything*," he said, rather ominously, Henry thought. They all sat uncomfortably for a few moments until Jane returned and handed her passport to Morris. He examined it closely for at least a half a minute and then handed it over to Harrison, who studied it himself for some time, making notes as he did so.

"You returned your stepmother's call at approximately five past four, Paris time. That was five past ten here, is that correct?" asked Morris, turning to Henry.

"You were here when the call came through," said Henry.

"So I was," said Morris. "Thank you. Now, Miss Casewait, after you completed your call you turned right around and returned to Charles de Gaulle Airport?"

"Well, no," said Jane. "The next available flight wasn't until the following noon. So I just waited and . . . thought. I had a lot to think about."

"Yes," said Morris, noncommittally. "You were in Paris," he continued, "to attend a meeting or convention of members of the organization you belong to or work for . . . ah, here it is, the International Society for the Promotion of Peace Through Serenity"?

"Yes," said Jane without blinking. "It was to be more of a seminar or exchange of ideas among the managers or heads of the different European branches of the society. I was there as an observer and, well, girl Friday or gofer as we'd probably call it here."

More like chief cook and bottle washer, thought Henry, who suspected that the maharishis were not above exploiting their followers, who were usually the sons and daughters of solidly middle-class parents.

"You left Paris at twelve," said Morris, "and arrived here approximately seven hours later at . . . " He considered his notes. "Two o'clock our time. Is that correct?"

"If you say so," said Jane, clearly beginning to tire of this line of questioning. "These time differences are always confusing, and I'm still suffering from jet lag, I'm afraid."

"I'm not even sure what day it is," said Jeanette. Morris looked at her sharply, Henry noticed.

"Yes," said Morris. "You must accept my apologies. This will only take a few minutes more. What sort of airplane did you travel in, Miss Casewait?"

"I really don't know. It was one of those big widebody things, a seven oh seven or a seven forty-seven; I can never tell the difference. They all look alike inside."

Morris nodded to Harrison, who made another note. Harrison had his work cut out for him, thought Henry. He hoped he didn't assign any of those follow-up calls to Bierson or Harley.

"And when you arrived you took a limousine to the local hotel and a cab from there. You arrived here at Mr. Wilnot's house at three thirty." Jane said yes and Henry, Erica, and Jeanette nodded in corroboration. Morris seemed to be finished. The next step, Henry supposed, would be to transfer all of these arrivals and departures to a blackboard in his office at the police station, where he could ponder them in the manner of several celebrated television cops. Did television writers study actual detectives, or did actual detectives study television? Henry tended to suspect the latter.

"I guess that will be all for now," said Morris, "except for Mr. Wilnot, of course, whom I will have to question about his little adventure yesterday." Henry's heart sank. He could only surmise what that blabbermouth Gianinni had told Morris. Something about his poking his nose into something that was none of his business, no doubt.

"I understand that your husband's funeral is tomorrow, Mrs. Casewait," said Morris, closing his notebook and turning to her.

"Yes," said Jeanette, "and I want to thank you again for your help in arranging things. I don't know how I could have managed otherwise." Henry must have looked hurt, because she quickly added, "Of course, Henry has been a rock and could have taken care of everything splendidly, but I didn't want to bother him with this in addition to all of the other things he has been doing." Henry nodded graciously, mollified, although he could not for the world think of anything he had done besides peeking at Casewait's financial statements and getting himself knocked on the head.

"I'll be leaving for California soon after the funeral," continued Jeanette. "With your permission, I understand," she added, glancing at Henry.

"There's really no need for you to stay here," said Morris. "And if we need you, we'll be in touch."

"There *is* one thing I'd like to talk with you about, Lieutenant," she said, and drew him away from Henry, who could guess what she was telling him.

"What do you suppose that was all about?" asked Jane, who joined Henry after retrieving her passport from Harrison.

"I would guess it's what he said it was," lied Henry. "Just routine." He glanced at Jane's passport as she stowed it in her shoulder bag. Something about that passport worried him, and he thought he knew why Morris had wanted to see it.

The last time Henry had talked to his daughter Gretchen, via transatlantic telephone—collect, of course—she had mentioned that she had visited Jane in Lausanne. She had only mentioned it in passing on the way to more important matters, namely money, for which she was as usual in desperate need, but there was one thing she said that had stuck in Henry's mind: Jane had somehow lost her passport, or had had it stolen, and was having a difficult time having it replaced. Henry remembered it because it had given Gretchen the opportunity for a diatribe against United States embassy officials all over the world who were either CIA agents or disgusting drunks and womanizers. This had struck Henry as a bit hypocritical, since a good case could be made that Gretchen and her companions were dope addicts and smugglers, or worse. The conversation had ended in the usual standoff, except Henry had sent her the money she had asked for.

"Why do you suppose he wanted to see your passport?" he asked.

"I have no idea," said Jane. "Maybe he wanted to check

my identity." Henry thought there was a note of contempt in her voice.

"Was that your new passport?"

"What?" she said, startled. "Why, no, as a matter of fact, it's my original one. Who told you I had lost my passport?" She looked at Henry suspiciously.

"Gretchen. She called about three months ago, to make sure she received her remittance."

"Oh," said Jane, laughing. "So that's it. I had lost my passport—or *thought* I had lost it, but it turned up again. And a good thing, too," she added. "I don't think I ever would have been able to get another from the embassy."

Henry was worried. He didn't like the line of questioning Morris had followed; the detective had been hard on both Jane and Jeanette, and obviously for some purpose. What the hell could he be thinking? And this business of the passport disturbed Henry even more. He found that he did not entirely believe Jane's story.

"Excuse me, Mr. Wilnot," said Detective Lieutenant Morris, joining them. "I wonder if you would be available for a short meeting tomorrow after Mr. Casewait's funeral. The sheriff would like to talk with you."

"Pardon me, Jane," said Henry, and then, turning his attention to Morris, "The sheriff? Don't *you* want to talk to me?" he asked.

"I think I have all the information I need right now." Gianinni and his big mouth, thought Henry. "And besides, the sheriff has a special interest in this particular aspect of the case."

"Oh?" said Henry, puzzled. "Don't *you* think it's important?" He had to restrain himself from feeling his head, which in shape, he imagined, roughly resembled that of the late Stan Laurel while he was wearing his bowler.

"Yes, of course, but it doesn't fit in with the line of investigation I am pursuing," said Morris with a decidedly self-satisfied air, or so it appeared to Henry.

"You know," said Henry, "it seems to me that you have this whole thing figured out."

"That may be, Mr. Wilnot, that may be. And now if you will excuse me? Miss Casewait?" he said, bowing slightly to Jane.

"What a polite policeman," said Jane after Morris and Harrison had said their good-byes to Jeanette and Erica.

"Hmm," said Henry, who was not at all impressed. He wondered if Lieutenant Morris had also studied theater at the police academy. A change of subject seemed in order, so he asked Jane, "What do you plan on doing after all of this is over?"

"Why, I'll go back to Europe, of course," she said. "It's the only place I've ever felt needed. I mean the society. I feel more at home there than I do here."

This saddened Henry. Why did his country, in which he felt so comfortable despite its absurdities, disappoint just about every young person he knew? Perhaps it really was, in spite of its seeming worship of youth, a country of old men.

"You know," he said, "you're going to come out of all this rather well fixed. Once the house is sold, unless you want to keep it—"

"Oh, no," said Jane quickly.

"—you may have more than two hundred thousand dollars to put into the bank, or do anything else with that you please. I hope you'll seek some financial advice."

"Oh, don't worry," she said eagerly. "I know what to do with it. We always need money." Henry had a vision of white-robed maharishis dancing in the streets of Paris when they heard the news, and felt even sadder than before.

The small group split up and went its separate ways, with Henry retreating to his den with enormous guilt at not having made directly for his workshed. He was too troubled to work, so he spent his time in fruitless conjecture as to what Morris and the sheriff were up to. He suspected that some politics were involved. Hadn't Scanlon warned him against Big Sam?

He considered phoning Miss Nathan, but could not think of an excuse for the call. All the necessary papers for probate had been delivered either through the mail or by messenger and everything seemed in good order on that front. He could call to tell her that the house was ready for viewing, since Jeanette and Jane had completed their sketchy inventory. He dialed the lawyer's number, but neither Scanlon nor Miss Nathan was in the office.

Henry decided to pay a visit to the local bank where Casewait had kept his checking and savings accounts. He might as well take steps to get them unfrozen or otherwise freed from whatever banks did with the money of deceased depositors.

"Ah, yes," said the young bank officer who came to greet Henry after he had made his business known. "My name is Snyder, and I believe I can help you." He was heavily mustached and, to Henry's eyes, bore a striking resemblance to Frank James. In Henry's day this young man wouldn't have been allowed within a mile of a bank, but here he was tending to a great part of the excess cash of the community. Now that Henry thought of it, it seemed that he was surrounded by what appeared to be desperadoes. Policemen looked like Mexican bandits, bank officers looked like Mississippi riverboat gamblers, and schoolteachers looked like both Sacco *and* Vanzetti, all due to the profusion of facial hair.

Henry produced his magical documents and his business was soon concluded. He was given temporary blank checks and was assured that he could withdraw cash from Casewait's accounts, if needed. "Did Mr. Casewait have a safety deposit box here?" asked Henry.

"No, I've checked on that," said Snyder. "We're the only bank in the area that has boxes, so if he didn't have one here I would doubt that he had one anywhere. He could have had one in the city, of course, if he was lucky enough to find a bank that had an empty one. I understand most of them have waiting lists."

"Oh?" said Henry, "I didn't realize that. What would you say this is, then?" he asked, handing Snyder the key he had found in Casewait's pool filter.

"It certainly looks like the key to a safe deposit box," said Snyder after examining it and returning it to Henry. "Of course, it could be a key to a box at a storage company. Quite a few of them have sprung up in the city as a result of the demand. Nobody wants anything valuable lying around their apartments down there."

Henry couldn't have agreed more. "Do you have any listing of these companies?" he asked.

"No, but I imagine the yellow pages is as good a guide as any. Do you want one of our people to do some research for you?"

"No, thank you," said Henry. "I think I can manage for myself. Well, good-bye, Mr. Snyder, and thank you for your help."

"Not at all," said Snyder. "Any time." Henry noticed that he was wearing fancy high-heeled cowboy boots with his three-piece suit.

12

ERICA HAD TAKEN it upon herself to make all of the arrangements for Casewait's funeral, revealing unexpected energy and a hitherto concealed talent for organization and detail. "It is the most I could do," she said—meaning, of course, the least she could do; her English was still unidiomatic. "And Jane has been such a help around the house, I just had to do something for them." As Henry had subsequently learned, it was Jane who was responsible for the spic-and-span appearance of his house. He had been disappointed to learn this; he had hoped that Erica had suddenly discovered the joys of housework in the manner of the actors in her beloved TV commercials.

The funeral went off smoothly. Except for its being at an hour that was considered early even by the standards of a community of commuters, the service in the anteroom of the crematorium had been simple and moving. There had been some difficulty in obtaining a clergyman—Casewait had never been known to set foot inside a local church—but Erica had called in some favors owed to her by the Methodist Church and secured the services of the youngest pastor in Christendom, so to speak, to read a few pages of the Book of Common Prayer over the . . . what? The memory of Joseph Casewait. (Casewait's ashes were not given to Jeanette until the mourners were ready to depart. Henry noted that the operators of the establishment were considerate enough not to attach the bill to the small box containing the simple urn.) The familiar words of the service touched Henry, and he felt more kindly disposed toward Casewait than he ever had while Joe had been alive. Of course, the Book of Common Prayer tended to have that effect: it could send witnesses away from the funeral of, say, Charles Manson feeling a deep sense of loss. Since Henry had to see the sheriff, he was unable to join the ladies in partaking of the funeral meats provided by the local McDonald's or Pizza Hut. As he was walking toward his car in the parking lot of the mortuary he was overtaken by a tall, elegantly stooped and impeccably tailored gentleman who, he guessed, was either a professor at one of the more distinguished local colleges or an advertising man of the old school. He proved to be the latter.

"Oh, hello there, Mr. Wilnot," he said somewhat breathlessly as he caught up to Henry. "I'm Ted Heath from Baines and Barlowe."

God, what a marvelous sentence, thought Henry. It was almost like saying "I'm Milton Friedman of the University of Chicago" or "I'm John Updike from Ipswich, Massachusetts."

"Yes, Mr. Heath," he said, stopping to receive his visitor. "What can I do for you?"

"I was just told that you're handling Mr. Casewait's estate. He used to work with us, and—"

"Oh, yes. I'm familiar with Baines and Barlowe. At least, I used to hear a lot about them from Joe."

"Hmm, yes," said Mr. Heath. "Then you know that he, uh, left us a while ago, but I'm not sure if you've come across any record of his pension plan with us, which was still in operation when he, uh, passed away."

"No, I haven's seen anything about it. I haven't really gone through his papers that thoroughly yet. I know that he had an insurance policy with your company that was still in force." Are they going to try to hedge on that? thought Henry, on his guard.

"No, this is something entirely different," said Mr. Heath. "This was actually a profit sharing plan, which you couldn't cash in until you'd retired or reached the age of sixty-five.

When Joe left the company, his share was automatically put in trust until such time as he was able to withdraw it. Now, of course, it becomes part of his estate."

"Really," said Henry, feeling a twinge of envy in spite of himself; he had put such corporate perks behind years ago. "Uh, how much does that entail, or don't you know?"

"I really don't know the exact figure, but I can assure you that it will be a nice bundle. You see, I double as a sort of office manager in our shop, and I was told by our comptroller, since I live around here, that I should get in touch with Casewait's heirs and clue them in. That was the first I'd heard that Joe was dead, as a matter of fact. Uh, terribly sorry, by the way," he added graciously. "I read about this service in the local papers and thought I might as well drop over on my way into the city."

"I see. Well, thank you, and I suppose your comptroller will be in touch with me, or shall I give him a call?"

"You'd better call him. He's up to his neck with this merger thing and it'll be some time before everything gets sorted out, but I do know that he wants to get this pension plan business out of the way fast."

"Oh?" said Henry. "What merger is that?"

Mr. Heath was well mannered enough not to show amazement at Henry's ignorance. "You don't work in the city then, I take it?"

"No," said Henry, "but I like to keep my ear to the ground."

"Baines and Barlowe has been taken over by Rodin and Michaels," said Mr. Heath in the same tone of voice he might have used to announce that the United States and the Soviet Union had signed a mutual assistance pact.

"Oh," said Henry, trying to look properly impressed. "Is this a hostile takeover, or whatever they call it?"

"Well, nobody's too happy about it, at least at our end. Anyway, it's one of the reasons we have to disperse all this cash that's sitting in our pension plan. The courts are pretty strict about that, and this is one case in which I agree with them. Otherwise Rodin and Michaels could make off with the whole kit and caboodle."

"You mean that Casewait would have collected on this thing even if he hadn't died?"

"Yeah, the lucky bastard—sorry. I mean he would have been a lucky bastard."

Henry had the distinct feeling that Mr. Heath, like the majority of mankind, did not think too highly of the late Joe Casewait.

"Look, Mr. Heath, I knew Joe Casewait pretty well, but I could never understand why he left Baines and Barlowe. Was he fired, or what?"

"Hmph. Well," said Mr. Heath, hedging. *De mortuis* . . . "

Ah, a fellow Latinist, thought Henry, and, if he knew anything about the advertising industry, a born gossip. "Yes, yes," he said, "I know, but Casewait went around saying that he told all of you down there to take your job and shove it."

"*What*?" said Mr. Heath. "He said *that*?"

"Not only that, but you begged him to stay."

"Well I'll be damned," said Mr. Heath.

"And that he took half of your clients with him," fibbed Henry. He knew that if there was one thing advertising men were sensitive about, it was the loss of clients.

"Oh, now wait a minute," said Mr. Heath. "If he said anything like that he was just plain lying. I'll tell you something, Mr. Wilnot, Joe Casewait was fired, sacked, thrown out on his ear." He fairly bristled with old-fashioned indignation. Henry half expected him to say, "Put that in your pipe and smoke it!"

"But why?" asked Henry. "I always thought he was the fair-haired boy down there."

"Well," said Mr. Heath, gaining control of himself. "I don't like to say—"

"He *was* a good adman, wasn't he? You've got to give him that."

"Oh, sure, he was good at the start—for quite a few years, in fact. But it just seemed that he was never satisfied with just doing a good job, serving the client. He always had to have something more."

"What do you mean?"

"It's hard to explain, really. For example, he was an account executive, right? And in our shop that means he had a copywriter and an art director working for him, getting his ads and his presentations in shape and things like that. But that wasn't enough for Joe. No, he had to write his own copy and even do his own layouts and roughs. And pretty soon he became his own art director and fired everybody else."

"Why would he do that? Wouldn't that mean more work for him? Joe was never what you'd call a workaholic," said Henry, wincing at the abominable coinage, which he would never normally use.

"No, it doesn't work like that. Being his own art director meant that Joe could hire freelancers, designers, photographers, models, whatever. In the end he probably had more people working for him than anybody else in the shop."

"But would that matter, if he got the job done, if he satisfied his clients?"

"That's just it."

"What is?"

"His clients."

"I don't get it."

Mr. Heath struggled with his discretion for a moment and then gave in. "Well, you see, Mr. Wilnot, Casewait specialized in accounts that were associated with what we call leisure-time activities. That sounds innocent enough, but leisure time includes booze and restaurants and show business, and *everything* that entails. All of these were areas Casewait was *very* interested in—in fact, too interested, some felt. Anyway, it became pretty obvious that he had crossed the line that separates customer and salesman."

"What does that mean?"

"No one knew for sure, but there were rumors of kick-backs, special favors, special arrangements made for one client by another client with Joe acting as middleman; that sort of thing. The rumors got so bad—and you know what rumors mean in this business—we had to get rid of him. And it may be true that he took some clients with him, but they were the type we would have given up gladly."

"Hmm, very interesting," said Henry, "very interesting. Well, look, I've got to be running. Thanks, Mr. Heath, and I'll be sure to get in touch with your comptroller. What was his name?"

"Here," said Mr. Heath. He took a business card from his wallet and scrawled a name on it. "I just hope we're all still there when you call," he added, not-so-jokingly.

"Oh, I'm sure everything will turn out all right," lied Henry, who was feeling a little better about his horse barn-work shed. At least it had a floor for a foundation.

The sheriff met with Henry in a conference room at police headquarters and put him at ease by seating him alone at one side of a bare table while he and two assistants faced him on the other. The assistants stood at each side of Big Sam and would lean down to him deferentially to receive commands or answer questions.

"Now, Mr. Wilnot," said the sheriff, "suppose you give us your version of just what happened to you the other day in the city."

"My version?" said Henry. "Is there another?"

"No, no," chuckled Big Sam, "we just want it from you firsthand. All we've had so far is the written report of the detective on the scene."

Henry proceeded to tell the same tale that he had given to Gianinni.

"You say this man was over six feet?" The sheriff broke in on Henry's narrative just as he was about to describe his coshing—or what he remembered of it besides the pain.

"Yes, probably about six two, and he was built like a free safety."

"And you had definitely seen him on the same train that you took to the city?"

"Yes."

"Do you think you could identify him?"

"I'm pretty sure I could even if he wasn't wearing that safari outfit. He shouldn't be difficult to pick up, should he? I mean, such a large man wearing an outfit like that should stand out even in a crowd."

"Mr. Wilnot," sighed the sheriff, "in the crowd this character hangs around in he wouldn't stand out even if he was dressed like one of the Three Musketeers.

"Anyway," added the sheriff, "we know who he is and it'll just be a matter of time before we collar him. We've been looking forward to getting something concrete we can pin on him."

"Who is he?" asked Henry, nervously. He didn't relish the idea of being the only witness to a crime committed by a six-foot-two linebacker.

"He calls himself Zawwada, but the police in the city have a sheet on him under the name Leroy Davis."

"Zawwada? What kind of a name is that?"

"He claims it comes from the Koran, but our experts tell us it's probably an Arab word out of the Congo region. It means something like 'provide' or 'supply,' but we think it may have something to do with the fact that he used to work out of the Port Authority Bus Terminal in the city. It could also mean 'procure.' "

"You mean he was a pimp."

"Probably, but his former profession is not what concerns us at the moment. You see, Mr. Wilnot," said the sheriff, leaning forward confidentially, "we know that Zawwada now works for one of the Italian families that control much of the organized crime in this area. We also think that your friend

Mr. Casewait was somehow connected with or employed by this same family."

"Employed!" said Henry. "You mean Joe Casewait actually *worked* for the Mafia? What did he *do* for them, for God's sake?"

"Mr. Wilnot," said Big Sam, "have you ever heard of a safe house?"

"Why, yes," said Henry. "I've read about them in spy stories. It's someplace run by a network in an enemy country where an agent can go if he's in trouble and has to hide out."

"Exactly," said the sheriff. "But in this case the network is organized crime and the agents are common criminals who either have to get rid of evidence or store stolen goods or money. What other businesses were located in this building where Mr. Casewait had his offices?"

"Mostly employment agencies, I guess."

"Perfect," said the sheriff. "Located in a high-crime area that is well patrolled by police. So any hood who thinks he's being tailed, or is carrying an illegal weapon, or who has to get rid of something he's just stolen from a shop or hotel room can just duck into this convenient building, dump whatever he wants to get rid of, and then wander around the corridors looking for an employment agency. If the police grab him, he's clean and has a perfect excuse for being there; he's looking for a job. You'd be surprised, Mr. Wilnot, how many hoods are out of work and desperately seeking employment."

"There *was* a safe in his office," said Henry reflectively.

"Sure," said the sheriff, "with damn good locks and big enough to hold an arsenal of handguns or a mint of dirty money that needs laundering."

"I see," said Henry. "But how can you be sure? The office was cleaned out, but that could have been done by any crooks, couldn't it?"

The sheriff smiled and again leaned forward confidentially. "What would you say, Mr. Wilnot, if I were to tell you that the gun that killed Mr. Casewait was the same weapon that was used in at least two unsolved gangland-style murders?"

"You've found the gun?" Henry nearly shouted.

"No, but we have the bullets. And they're about as close a match as I've ever seen."

Scanlon's warning to Henry crossed his mind: *Watch out for Big Sam; he's got the Mafia on his mind*, or words to that effect. Could the sheriff be bluffing for some reason, trying to get Henry to reveal more than he knew?

"And your neighbor Mr. Casewait," continued the sheriff, "doesn't—didn't seem the sort who would go around pumping lead into cheap hoods and then stuffing their bodies into the trunks of cars. But he just might have been the sort who would run a safe house and launder money or get rid of hot guns."

"I don't know," said Henry, unconvinced. "It's pretty hard to believe. After all, I knew the man. . . ." Which should make it that much easier to believe, thought Henry.

"We'll give him the benefit of the doubt and say that he didn't know how the guns were used, or even if they *were* used. But there *is* the definite connection between his death and a gun used by a hit man or just a plain gangland killer like your Zawwada here."

"Then you're saying that Joe Casewait was the target of a hit man or a Mafia killer."

"It looks that way," said the sheriff. "Which brings us to another little matter, Mr. Wilnot." He held his hand over his shoulder and one of his assistants placed a piece of paper in it. The sheriff studied it closely, occasionally glancing across the table at Henry. He broke the silence with "You're familiar with this, aren't you, Mr. Wilnot?"

"Yes," said Henry. "I believe that's the note to me that was found with Mr. Casewait's will."

"Yes," said the sheriff. "Very interesting. What was your impression of it when you first read it?"

"Well, considering the fact that Joe had just been shot, it struck me that when he wrote it he must have felt that he was in danger of his life."

"Exactly," said the sheriff—evidently it was one of his favorite expressions. "Now, Mr. Wilnot, there are some things that we don't understand about this letter, and perhaps you could clear them up for us."

"I'll do the best I can."

"There's a reference here to his being done in by the citizenry—"

"Or the booze," interrupted Henry.

"Yes," said the sheriff, giving him a fishy glance. "Is there anything else you can tell us about that, Mr. Wilnot?"

"I don't think he was referring to anything or anyone specific. It was just his manner of speaking—or that is, of writing."

The sheriff went back to studying the letter. Henry hoped that he would ask what the reference to the local Lestrade meant, but he was disappointed. The sheriff leaned forward ominously. "Who is this half crazed Wop he refers to?" he said sharply.

Henry was taken by surprise, but then he remembered the passage. Oh, my God! he thought.

"I believe that is a reference to Catullus," said Henry.

The sheriff absorbed this, then sat back in his chair and looked up at the man on his left, an eyebrow raised quizzically. The assistant shook his head and shrugged his shoulders, sort of a visual double negative. The sheriff looked at the other man. He too shook his head. "Casellas, Costellos—no Catulluses that I know of." He thought for a moment. "Maybe in Jersey."

The sheriff turned back to Henry. "Just who is this Catullus?" he asked accusingly.

"He was a Roman poet," said Henry. He did not dare to smile.

The sheriff stared at him. A slight flicker of the eyes, a

momentary wavering of the steely gaze, indicated to Henry that Big Sam might—just might—have realized that he had been made a fool of. And Big Sam did not strike Henry as the sort of man who relished being made a fool of. Henry felt more threatened than ever.

Surprisingly the sheriff said, "Can you quote something he has written?"

Henry thought awhile, and then extemporized:

"Passer mortuus est meae puellae.
Vivamus, mea Lesbia, atque amemus.
Ad clara Asiae volemus urbes.
Phasellus ille, quen videtis, hospites.
Et tu, frater, ave atque vale."

He then sat back, rather pleased with himself. Actually, what he had recited was a collection of memorable—or, at least, easily memorized—tag lines from the more famous poems. They did, however, make a kind of sense:

My lovely girl's sparrow is dead.
Come, my Lesbia, let us live and let us love.
Fly to our fine Aegean cities.
This little boat, my guests, just look at it!
And you, brother, hail and farewell.

So Henry was prepared to translate if called upon. Still, he couldn't help wishing he had a pony.

The sheriff absorbed the ill-pronounced Latin noncommittally. He looked once again to the assistant on his left. The man shrugged. "It's not Sicilian," he said defensively. The sheriff could barely conceal his contempt for him.

"All right, Mr. Wilnot," he said, turning again to Henry. "Now I must ask you if there is anything else you can tell us about Mr. Casewait or about the circumstances of the attack upon you, that you think might be of some help to us in our investigation. Anything at all, Mr. Wilnot, no matter how small."

Henry did not want to tell the sheriff about Casewait's key, at least not until he consulted with Morris or Scanlon, so he said nothing.

"I should warn you," continued the sheriff, "that if Zawwada—or, more precisely, his employers—did not discover what they were looking for in Mr. Casewait's office or on your person, they will try to get it again, whatever it may be."

Henry was slightly unnerved. Did Big Sam know that he had something, was hiding something? And did Henry have any responsibility to tell him about it? He wished that the lines of jurisdiction in the county were more precisely drawn.

"Frankly, Mr. Wilnot, there is nothing we would like more than to catch Zawwada in the midst of an act of . . ." Here the sheriff treated Henry to a pause of the type that used to be called pregnant. "Violence. But not at your expense, of course." The sheriff seemed to be chuckling to himself as he rose to his feet.

On this chilling note, Henry surmised that the interview was over and that he was free to go, which he did, with alacrity.

Later that day, Henry sat in his study pondering Casewait's mysterious key. He now had no doubt that it was a key to a safe deposit box somewhere. But where? One would expect that it would bear some sort of identifying mark on it, but then that was the point of a safe deposit box, wasn't it? No one should know about it but the depositor.

He turned the key in his hand, looking at it against the light, and then he noticed that someone had moved Casewait's—now his—Loeb's Classics. In fact, someone had cleaned his whole study, which usually had the look of studied shabbiness that one associates with absentminded college professors. The Loebs had been removed from his desk and were now neatly stacked on top of a low bookcase—which, Henry noticed, had been dusted. The books in the bookcase also appeared to have been dusted and were neatly aligned with their spines flush with the edge of the shelves, a formerly unheard of occurrence. Henry liked his books in disarray, indicating a tireless and sometimes frantic quest for knowledge by their owner. Erica couldn't have done it—it was well known that her idea of dusting was to lift up a table lamp or ashtray and blow under it—so it must have been Jane, Henry decided. As much as he liked the girl, he had to allow that sometimes she went too far. He remembered her once sifting the sand he was using to mix cement for a retaining wall he was building against the encroaching wilderness at the side of his house. He had chided her for being too fussy, but perhaps she had been right; the wall had crumbled some years ago.

Henry returned the key to his pocket and tried to dismiss it from his mind. He would consult with Morris or Scanlon about it tomorrow. Just now he was troubled enough to be unable to pursue the course that events seemed to demand. He had not done any work in days; he had been viciously attacked by a black Man Mountain Dean; he had in his possession what might be a crucial piece of evidence; he had an estate to settle and a house to get off his hands. And he had two female adults practically in residence in his house who didn't seem as anxious to move out as they insisted they were. He could hear the women in the kitchen, no doubt consuming more of the gallons of coffee they brewed all day.

"*Eheu*!" he sighed. The old Latin cry brought his attention back to his Loebs. What a treasure! How much Horace did he have? he wondered. He got up from his cracking leather chair, which not even Jane could do anything about, and went to the bookcase to examine the gleaming red and gold volumes. He had plenty of Horace, he saw, and thought of the dismay that would bring to most schoolchildren. Latin was coming back, he had heard, and he couldn't approve more. Let the little stinkers suffer! he thought. The subjunctive mood crossed his mind and he shuddered; perhaps he was being too harsh. When his own children had gone to school they made up their own exams and graded each other. *And* had critiques of their teachers instead of exams. If they had had to memorize a paradigm, they would have gone into shock. Strangely, however, his daughter now spoke excellent French and German and his son spoke Spanish like a native Los Angeleno.

Henry ran his eye down the stack of volumes until he found what he realized he had actually been looking for all along: Catullus. Wielder of the stateliest measure ever molded by the lips of man, and half crazed Wop. O Montovano, thought Henry, rather taken with the antique mood, what has brought you back to me after all these years? A cheap wisecrack by a deceased libertine and the befuddlement of a suburban gangbuster. He extracted the volume from its stack and collapsed into his chair.

Henry cracked the book and it fell open to the great poem 101, Catullus's memorial to his brother, dead in the Troad. Tucked into the binding was a plain white business card. A bookmark? Henry wondered if Casewait had actually consulted the poem before writing his note; certainly even as indifferent a scholar as Casewait would know how to spell *ave atque vale*. He looked at the card.

CONSOLIDATED STORAGE
Lockers • Safes • Safety Deposit Boxes

At the bottom was an address in the city—below Twenty-third Street, just west of Fifth Avenue—and a telephone number. On the back was written a number—34—in ink. Henry mulled this information over in his mind. There was no doubt about it: Casewait had stored something in a safe deposit box, and it wasn't one of your run-of-the-mill and eminently respectable boxes pushed by your stodgy local banker, either.

Henry put a call through to Scanlon, to find predictably

that the great man was not available; he asked to be put through to Miss Nathan, and her cool voice soon greeted him.

"What can I do for you, Mr. Wilnot?"

"What's the law on opening the safe deposit box of a person who's been shot?" asked Henry. He went on to give her a brief explanation of the key, without telling her how it had come into his possession.

"The same as with any other deceased persons," she said. "You have to open it in the presence of an officer of the bank. The presence of a lawyer wouldn't hurt, if you're worried about it, but it really isn't necessary." Henry thought he detected a note of regret in her voice. All those fees lost.

"But his isn't a box in a bank," he said. "It's in a storage company or something in the city. And, frankly, it sounds like a pretty suspicious place."

"How do you mean, suspicious?"

"Well, as I understand it, ever since the kids and the terrorists started using all the coin lockers in town to plant their bombs in, there's no place for people to stash things—you know, illegally, or at least on the sly. So a lot of these seamy storage houses have started providing lockers, only they call them safe deposit boxes."

"Oh, really?" said Miss Nathan. "I hadn't heard of that." She was decidedly cool. Probably didn't like his tone when he referred to the infant bombers, Henry decided.

"I really don't know how to advise you," she said after a pause. "I imagine it's like any other piece of property in storage. Your letter testamentary should be enough to get it for you, but if what you say is true, chances are all that you'll need is the key. Anyway, I'll check it out for you as soon as I can. I have to show some houses this afternoon. In fact, I'm late right now."

"How're you making out with Casewait's house?" asked Henry.

"Didn't Mr. Scanlon tell you?"

"No, I haven't spoken to him in some time."

"Well," said Miss Nathan confidentially, "I think we have a buyer. His name's Birmingham, and he's a scientist who's been transferred to———" She named one of the huge corporations whose green- and blue-tinted glass box structures littered the surrounding hills and woods like discarded children's blocks. "And he's willing to pay *cash*!"

"Why in the world would he want to do that?" asked Henry. His own tax deductions for interest payments on his mortgage were the only thing that had kept him barely solvent all these years.

"Well, mortgages aren't that easy to get, but I think I can talk him into taking over the existing mortgage, and then a second mortgage on that, since the first is almost paid up. That would be all right with you, wouldn't it?"

"Yes, but—"

"I'm sorry, but I really have to go," she said. "I'm hours late already. Mr. Scanlon will be in touch with you soon. G'bye."

"—When will I get to meet this Mr. What's-his-name?" Henry finished, talking to the dial tone.

He dialed the police and waited. After about the twelfth ring he was about to hang up when the laconic voice of either Harley or Bierson came through. Didn't those two ever go off duty? thought Henry, or was it just his imagination? He asked for Detective Lieutenant Morris, only to be told that he was off on an investigation to the north of the county.

Henry hung up and wondered what to do with himself. He stood looking out the window. There was Casewait's house and there was the forest primeval. And somewhere out there were policemen who were keeping him under surveillance, as the saying goes. He knew for a certainty that either Harley or Bierson was at the police station, so they couldn't *both* be detailed to watch his house. Somehow he found this fact comforting—except that it raised the possibility that there was only *one* policeman out there, and he was either Harley *or* Bierson. With this disturbing thought lingering in his mind, he decided to try to do some work. Tomorrow there would be time to settle the business of the key. Perhaps he would just give it to Morris, who could then dispatch the blue van to the city to pick up whatever was in the safe deposit box. But the blue van belonged to the sheriff, and Henry definitely did not like the idea of anything having to do with Casewait's shooting falling into the hands of Big Sam.

13

THAT NIGHT HENRY had a Shakespearean dream in which Casewait, clad in a suit of armor, came clanking toward him across a vast plain littered with corporate-headquarters cubes of glass. "The key . . . the key," he seemed to be saying. "How obvious can you get?" thought Henry, even in sleep rebuking his dream mechanism. Then either Harley or Bierson leapt from nowhere and began beating Casewait on the helm with his nightstick, making a tremendous racket. Henry started awake.

Erica slumbered beside him. There was no moon and Henry could barely make out the windows in the opposite wall. The house was absolutely still, and empty, except for the two of them. Jeanette and Jane had decided to go into the city and treat themselves to some shopping and dinner and a show. They were staying the night in a hotel—Jeanette somehow had ways of getting theater tickets and hotel rooms on the spur of the moment—and would return the next day. The luminous dial of the clock on the night table showed it to be ten minutes to two.

Henry had heard something: it had come from his work shed; he was sure of it. It sounded as though something metallic had fallen to the floor. Henry tried to picture the interior of the shed. He could not recall anything light enough to fall to the floor due to, say, a window shade blowing against it. Wait a minute—there was the tin cup that he used to drink from when he administered himself a belt of booze to unblock. Henry did not keep a glass in the shed because he felt you had to clean a glass every so often, but a tin cup never needs cleaning. He had left it on the manuscript table next to the door, he remembered. Now, what would cause it to fall to the floor? He lay on his back, staring at the ceiling he could not see, and pondered the question for a few moments.

It must be the raccoons, he decided, even though he hadn't heard or seen any yet this year. They had once driven him nearly to distraction, using his garbage cans as an all-night cafeteria, where they came and went like a bunch of unemployed actors. He had finally bought one of those trash cans that has a screw-on lid, like a gigantic peanut butter jar. The night after he had installed it he looked out of his bedroom window to observe a big old fellow standing on his hind legs and calmly unscrewing the top of the can, using the same graceful, two-armed motion as the rear-wheel man on a hook and ladder.

That must be it, thought Henry, the raccoons. Except he was positive that he had locked the door to the shed, because he remembered having trouble with the old bicycle-type padlock and had specifically reminded himself to buy a new one. Hmm, thought Henry, this calls for a new line of thinking. But what? Perhaps some action might help.

He got out of bed and padded in his bare feet across the rug to the nearest window. He carefully opened the casement-type screen—something told him to be as quiet as possible—and leaned out into the night, his ears all but flapping. He could barely make out his own garage, which was situated at the end of the long blacktop driveway that badly needed resealing. He could not see his work shed at all. There was not a sound, even the insects had ceased their din and called it a night, but Henry knew that someone was out there.

He held his breath for a full fifteen seconds and listened so hard that he felt like a radar transmitter sending out radio waves that would soon bounce back at him. Someone coughed in the darkness out back of the garage. Henry's scalp tingled and his heart began to flutter inside his pajama top. He wondered if his long overdue heart attack was about to announce itself.

Henry withdrew his head from the window and stumbled to a wing chair in the corner of the room. He sat in the darkness for what must have been a full minute until his vital signs began to get back on the polygraph belt. He suddenly had a happy thought: perhaps either Harley or Bierson was making his rounds, checking over both the empty and the sleeping house.

Fat chance! If either was on duty, he most certainly would not leave his patrol car, and was most likely asleep. No, whoever was out there was awake and alert.

Henry had a shotgun in the attic, a relic of the days when he had tried to interest Harold in the outdoor life, but he knew there were no shells for it in the house. After Harold had indicated in no uncertain terms that for him it was the arts or nothing, Henry had abandoned any attempts at leading an outdoor existence. What he wouldn't give for a deer rifle, or even one of those pellet guns that were so popular in towns without leash laws.

His eyes had now become more accustomed to the dark, and he searched the room for some means of self-defense, but there was nothing in it out of the ordinary except Harold's electric guitar, amplifier, microphone, and speakers, which Henry had moved from the guest room to make room for Jane when she had first arrived.

Henry sighed. What was he excited about? All he had to do was call the police—only by the time his call got through the house could be ransacked and he and Erica brutally expunged. In fact, the invader would be able to go about his work quite calmly while Henry stood by exasperatedly with the phone to his ear.

Or he could simply turn on all the lights and he and Erica could start screaming at the top of their lungs and beating pots and pans together until they raised the sleeping patrolman watching the house, if indeed there actually was anyone from the police out there. He had only Gianinni's word that the house was being watched. He had never actually *seen* any uniforms lurking about the place.

Somehow this last alternative did not appeal to him. For one thing, Erica was well launched on her nightly journey, and he knew that it would take longer to rouse her than it would take to get the police on the phone. For another, it was just not—well, dignified. Also, he was curious, even though he had a good idea of who it was out there. And he was, finally, vindictive. He still had a very painful lump on his head, which had been given to him quite gratuitously by a minion of organized crime, as Big Sam might say, and he didn't like it.

Still, he thought, the idea of light and noise wasn't a bad one. Years ago Harold had installed a spotlight on the corner of the house, which Henry could use in his fight against the raccoons. Harold had run a control cable to Henry's bedroom, from which a beam of light could be directed to almost anywhere at the rear of the house. Henry groped behind a bookcase until he found the pistol-grip arrangement that directed the spotlight and then pulled out the extension cord with the simple on-off switch. He hadn't used it for years, but as far as he knew it still worked.

He next sneaked across the room and gathered up Harold's microphone, amplifier, and speakers and brought them over to the window. He then collected the guitar and all of the other plugs and wires that he had once vaguely understood, and quietly placed them on the floor next to a wall socket. Henry had assisted Harold in putting all of this together years ago, and he felt he still knew the drill, as they used to say in the army. He unscrambled some of the cords and plugged in a connection here and there until he finally had things arranged as he remembered them. The main plug was free, anyway, and that was the important thing. He had the presence of mind to check that an adapter was on the three-prong plug. If it hadn't been there he would have had to creep downstairs in the dark and swipe one from the dishwasher. Living in an old house had its drawbacks.

If there was one thing Henry understood about the electrical amplification of sound, it was that it never worked the first time. In his experience, whenever you activated an amplifier, it screeched long and earsplittingly until you removed or disconnected the microphone. The cause was feedback. Harold had explained it all to Henry—it had something to do with the input of a signal into a microphone from the output of the same system—but all Henry knew was that it made one hell of a noise, and that any prudent person would keep the volume on the amplifier as low as possible while setting up his equipment.

Henry set the amplifier as loud as it would function. He then placed a speaker on the windowsill, facing outward, and took the microphone, which he had detached from its stand, and placed it directly in front of the speaker. He gathered up the spotlight controls in one hand, and the main plug for the amplifying system in the other, and once again leaned out the window.

Silence, except for the sweet wind gently kissing the trees. Fine, Henry thought to himself.

The tall doors to Henry's garage were painted white, and what on a moonlit night would appear to be a shadow was moving slowly in front of them. Henry turned the spotlight control in his hand until he thought he had the actual light pointed toward the garage, and then, with a silent prayer, plugged in the amplifier and switched on the spotlight.

Henry had been intrigued by a news story he once read about a woman in Weehawken, New Jersey, who decided to do some ironing on the night of the great power blackout of November 1965. She lived in an apartment with a magnificent view of almost the whole of Manhattan, and on that particular night the sight was so impressive that she moved her ironing board in front of her window so that she could enjoy the magical panorama while working. She plugged in her iron, and at that exact moment all of New York flickered and went dark. The poor woman fainted dead away. She thought she had blown the biggest fuse in the world.

What happened when Henry plugged in the amplifier was entirely different. He believed that he had tapped into some source of energy residing deep within the bowels of the earth. The spotlight went on with a sharp crackling sound—but it wasn't a spotlight: Harold had replaced it with a floodlight years ago, and it bathed all of the area around the garage in an eerie blue-white light. Illuminated against one of the garage doors was Zawwada, who had staggered back against the door and stood in the classic stance of the escaping convict, arms outstretched on either side with palms pressed against the wall.

At the same time there arose from the speaker on the windowsill a howl, a screech, a shriek, a scream unlike anything Henry had ever heard before. About a mile away, all the dogs at Hardstone Kennels, receiving ultrasonic waves far in advance of those detectable by the human ear, awoke as one and began howling, barking, yapping, yelping, snarling, returning this horrendous cacophony along the same freakish acoustical lines to just outside Henry's window. Erica sat bolt upright in bed and shouted, "*Gross Gott—!*" and began screaming at the top of her range, which was considerable, since she had been trained in the finest of German music schools. This startled Henry as much as anything else, since he had never seen her arise from a sleeping position; he was usually up ages before her.

Down in the driveway, Zawwada had recovered and pulled an evil-looking Schnauzer from his belt and hastily fired two shots at the floodlight. Henry ducked and heard with a sinking heart the rounds bury themselves in the loose shingles outside his window. Who was going to repair those? he thought as he pulled out the plug to the amplifier. A comparative silence set in.

"What the hell was *that*?" said a voice somewhere on the far side of Casewait's house. Lights went on, a car started, roared into reverse, and then screeched forward and careered up Henry's driveway. Zawwada had taken off immediately after firing his shots and must have headed toward the back of Henry's property, which ended in a swollen creek that might more properly be called a swamp.

Two uniformed police officers blundered into the light in front of Henry's garage. "Are you all right, Mr. Wilnot?" Harley or Bierson shouted.

"I'm all right," said Henry, leaning out of thc window and pointing toward the back of his property. "He went that way! Go get him!"

The officers were having none of that, so they rushed back to their car and radioed for reinforcements. Henry collapsed into his chair and looked across at Erica. She was lying down once again, and had pulled the sheet over her head. Had she gone back to sleep, thinking that what had happened was merely an especially noisy nightmare?

"Erica?" he said tentatively.

She stirred slightly.

"Erica?" he said again. "Are you all right?"

"I vant to go back to Chermany," she said from under the covers.

14

ZAWWADA WAS CAPTURED easily as dawn broke. He was found huddled beside a fallen tree in the swamp behind Henry's house. The sheriff, who had taken over the search, was ecstatic. Whether through taste or compassion, he had declined to use bloodhounds, but his men easily turned up the cowering intruder, of whom it could truly be said that he was a shell of his former self.

"Took him without a shot being fired," the sheriff proudly told the press. "On his own turf, it probably would have cost us two or three dead and God knows how many wounded." The sheriff then looked the television cameramen and newspaper photographers squarely in their lenses and carefully enunciated, "This is the most important single arrest ever made in the fight against organized crime in this county. And not the last, by any means," he added as significantly as he could.

Henry was just as satisfied that Big Sam had failed to mention Henry's own part in the affair except in passing. He didn't relish the idea of Zawwada's cohorts swarming out of the city bent on revenge. Big Sam made only one mention of the Casewait case, as it was called in the newspapers, but that was significant: "I believe this case can now be closed," he said, "at least as far as my office is concerned. We of course shall aid the local police if they request our help, but I think I can safely say that they should have no trouble in wrapping it up themselves." He refused to elaborate, implying that it would endanger the prosecution's case if he said anything further. Which, Henry had to admit, was absolutely true. A lawyer like Scanlon could get Zawwada off by requesting and probably getting a mistrial just on the strength of what the sheriff had already said.

Henry put through a call to Detective Lieutenant Morris and after the usual delay was told that the detective was off on another investigation. Henry had no reason to doubt it. There had been so much concurrent local, national, and international terrorism, brutality, kidnapping, aggression, and murder that every law-enforcement agency in the world was worn to a frazzle. This was one of the reasons the Casewait case had not attracted much attention from the media. The poor overworked wretches simply didn't have the manpower or the time and space to cover the death under peculiar circumstances of a suburban reprobate. All of which was perfectly all right with Henry. But now that Big Sam was no longer interested in Casewait's murder, it seemed to Henry that he himself and Morris were the only people who had the least concern about the case—and he wasn't even too sure about Morris.

Henry decided to clear up the business of Casewait's key himself. Big Sam would not be interested, Morris never seemed to be available, and Scanlon was probably off somewhere pleading the civil rights of some child molester. Rather than submit himself to the torture of riding a commuter train twice within the same week, he climbed into his ancient Volkswagen, and after waving good-bye to Erica, who was sleepily groping her way onto the back porch, he set off for the great city.

If nothing else, the automobile permits one to maintain his integrity, which is probably why people still cling to it in spite of oil shortages and ruinous expenses. Henry sailed along the parkways, inviolate and alone in his metal cocoon, and pondered his situation. It was not good, he decided. After the pandemonium of the previous night had dissipated, Erica indicated that she was going to make good on her vow to return to Germany. She had made such a vow many times as the result of the little rough spots that occur in any marriage, and had actually made the trip two or three times. She usually stayed away two weeks, until the badgering of that ancient *Wirtschaftswunderarchitekten*, her father, sent her literally flying back to Henry's arms. Nevertheless, these separations pained Henry more than he cared to admit, and he did not look forward to them.

The settlement of Casewait's affairs did not seem to be making any progress, and Scanlon and Miss Nathan had made themselves scarce again. He had heard or read somewhere that the probate of even the simplest of wills could take as long as a year, and this depressed him even further. He had not done any real work since Casewait had been shot, and he knew that he would not be able to keep up his normal rate of production with this thing hanging over his head. He also owed it to Jeanette to free all of Casewait's assets and to sell the house as soon as possible, since she seemed about to enter into a new phase of her life, and it would not do to have her former husband's affairs as a constant pull at her new happiness. Well, he thought, at least Miss Nathan seemed to be making some progress with marketing the house. It still bothered him slightly that he had not listed it with a proper real estate broker, but what the hell; he couldn't do everything, and you had to trust somebody sometime. And besides, Miss Nathan seemed chillingly efficient, and he had the feeling that when it came to haggling over a price, she would do a better job of it than most.

Henry had been so engrossed in his own problems that he had not noticed that he had passed under the approaches to the George Washington Bridge and was now on the West Side Highway. A few teeth-rattling jolts caused by the potholes that pitted the patched and cracked roadbed brought him awake to the fact that he was speeding toward, was indeed already in, the city. He became wary and switched to the outside lane, where he felt safer than he did in the two inside speedway lanes. But this exposed him to the cars that came rocketing out of the entries on his right. You simply could not win in this town; the whole place was designed to torment him, he thought.

The traffic had suddenly thickened, as cars began materializing from all sides. Henry eyed each passing motorist uneasily; he thought once that he glimpsed a white-hunter's hat, but he could have been mistaken, since the car driven by its wearer shot past him at sixty or seventy miles per hour. What had Big Sam said? The characters Zawwada hangs out with, he could dress like one of the Three Musketeers and no one would notice him. Henry was painfully reminded of this as he caught a glimpse of the driver of a vintage fifties Cadillac that sped past him at a speed he would have thought impossible for such an ancient vehicle. He could have sworn that the driver was wearing a plumed hat.

Henry turned off the highway at the Seventy-ninth Street exit and took Ninth Avenue downtown. His attention was riveted to the road, since any deviation from his steady course in the middle lane could spell disaster, what with cars and taxis weaving in and out of lanes with no regard for the sanctity of life. He ran several red lights, since he knew that if he did not he could cause a massive pileup of at least ten cars behind him, the drivers of which did not know from traffic signals.

He finally arrived at the joyless, bleak and arid industrial section of the West Side that lies below Twenty-third Street and had no trouble in finding a parking space near the premises of Consolidated Storage Company. He locked his car—indeed, he would have thrown a chain around it and fastened it to the nearest tree if he had had a chain, or if there had been a tree to fasten it to—and looked around him. Human habitation in this area was sparse as compared with the teeming reaches of the rest of the island, which made it eerier than Central Park at night. Henry found the building he was looking for, a depressing pile of tin and masonry probably erected during the palmy days of the turn of the century and now in the last stages of erosion, and entered into a lobby that was unrelievedly antiseptic and sleazy at the same time. He located the number of Consolidated Storage and pressed the elevator button. After a great deal of humming and clanging, the elevator door opened, and Henry, pausing a moment to make sure that all of the innards of the vehicle had settled and come to terms with themselves, entered cautiously.

The offices of Consolidated Storage consisted of the usual waiting area with a chair and a table with a lamp on it, and an aperture through which one could speak to a receptionist who wore harlequin eyeglasses and chewed gum. After stating his name and purpose he was clicked and buzzed through several doors until he found himself in the closet-size office of one Mr. Cardolla, a sharp-faced man with a pencil-thin mustache. Mr. Cardolla was clad in chalk-striped gray flannel pants and vest and appeared to fit everyone's idea of the small-time grifter.

As Henry explained his business, Mr. Cardolla seemed to ooze distrust. "I don't know," he said, examining Henry's letter testamentary. "We've never had anything like this before. We're kinda new at this." He looked up at Henry with a suspicious glance. "Aren't you supposed to have a lawyer with you? That's the way the banks do it, isn't it?"

"Not necessarily," said Henry, with his newfound expertise. "Usually just a bank officer is present, and in this case you're the equivalent of a bank officer, aren't you?"

"Huh? Me?" said Cardolla, startled. He appeared to turn the idea over in his mind for a moment, and was not altogether displeased with it. "Yeah, that's right. Heh-heh. Me, a bank officer." He became quite genial. "Well, okay, if you've got the key."

"You could check with the city police, if you like," said Henry. "There's a detective named Gianinni who could—"

"No, no," said Cardolla quickly, "there's no need for that. Now, what was the number?"

"Thirty-four," said Henry, handing the key to Cardolla,

who examined it and then went into an adjoining room that was even smaller than the one they were in. He reemerged after a few moments, holding two keys aloft triumphantly. "Okay," he said. "Let's go. Just follow me."

Henry dutifully followed the spiffy figure through a few more doors and into a large and drafty loft filled with movers' boxes and crates of various sizes. Cardolla led Henry to a corner that was curtained off from the rest of the barnlike room, and pulled aside a flap in the curtain.

"Here it is. Just like a bank, heh-heh." Cardolla still seemed beguiled by the idea of his being the overseer of the public's money supply. He went to a low pile of boxes of graduated dimensions and knelt down beside the lowest group, which were slightly larger than the average-size briefcase. He located number thirty-four, inserted both keys, turned the locks, and deftly withdrew the box, tucking it under his arm. "Here we go," he said and led Henry to a curtained booth opposite the stack of boxes. He placed the box he was carrying on a wide shelf, opened it slightly to show Henry it was unlocked, but did not look inside. He was the soul of discretion.

"It's all yours," said Cardolla, extending an open palm toward the box. Henry wondered if he was expected to grease it—the palm—but decided not to, since Cardolla, with his newfound dignity, might take offense. One did not tip bank officers.

Henry stepped into the booth. "Do you want to examine the contents with me?" he asked.

"No!" exclaimed Cardolla, suddenly wary. "I don't wanna know *nothin*!" he said hastily. "Look, I'm gonna go back into my office and see if you owe anything on this—I guess you won't want this box no more, right?—and you just collect your property or whoever's it is and then check in with me. Okay? I'm right across the loft. It's the only way out, so we won't miss each other."

"Fine," said Henry, "I won't be more than a minute."

Cardolla, the erstwhile bank officer, reverted to type and scurried back to his office like one of the rats that undoubtedly infested the loft.

Henry drew the curtain of the booth, even though so far as he could tell there was not another soul in the loft; he just felt furtive. He raised the lid of the box, revealing a briefcase that fit snugly into the metal container. He took it out, laid it flat on the shelf, and sprang the catches. The briefcase was unlocked—Who locks briefcases? he thought idly—and raised the top.

Henry sincerely believed that charge cards were one of the great innovations in the history of mankind's quest for comfort and ease of mind, and he seldom carried any more cash than was needed for his immediate purposes; but he was of an age and a generation that had not entirely forgotten the look and feel of money, the intense excitement that came over one merely in the proximity of large amounts of moolah. He therefore gasped in astonishment at what he saw.

The briefcase was about three and one half inches deep, and had been crammed full with thirteen stacks of bank notes. With slightly trembling fingers, Henry prised one of the stacks loose. It consisted of five neatly banded bundles made up of hundreds, fifties, and twenties, nothing smaller, in an artful combination of used and new bills. Henry flipped hurriedly through one bundle and calculated roughly that it contained four thousand dollars. Five times four is twenty, and twenty times thirteen is two hundred sixty. The briefcase contained over a quarter of a million dollars, probably more than Henry could earn in the rest of his working life—unless of course some mass-market-paperback or television deal came through.

Henry snapped the briefcase shut and left the small cubicle that resembled the polling booth where he regularly voted against his town's school budget. He walked briskly through the flap in the outer curtain and across the lofty room to the doorway that led to Cardolla's control center.

He was still in a state of mild shock, but he managed to maintain a cool and businesslike air as he paid Cardolla twenty dollars for some charge that the man undoubtedly made up on the spot. Henry signed something—it looked like a release, but he was too inwardly agitated to read it—and fled the offices of Consolidated Storage.

He was tempted to take the stairs instead of the elevator, but he knew that muggers lurked in stairways, and this was hardly the time to get mugged! The elevator arrived and conveyed him safely if excruciatingly slowly to street level. After furtive glances up and down the nearly deserted street, Henry made his way to his parked car. He was a study in nonchalance, except for his boxer's crouch, his catlike movements, and the rapid shifting of his eyes from side to side.

15

QUITE A FEW years before, when Henry was still commuting to the city, he had run into an old friend named Hendrickson who was rushing to catch the same train as he was. Hendrickson had been briefly employed by a publishing house Henry had worked for many years previously, but, being a bright lad and a quick study, had soon figured out that publishing was a game for losers and had fled back to the shelter of academic elms, where he perceived that a bundle was to be made.

Hendrickson soon obtained his doctorate and for some years had been teaching at one of the city's more prestigious universities. In his search for a subject for his doctoral thesis, he had lighted upon an obscure British poet, a contemporary of Rupert Brooke, Wilfred Owen, and other doomed young men, who had somehow managed to survive the Great War and had led the exemplary life of a country gentleman until he was pitched into a stone quarry by his favorite mare, as so often happens to country gentlemen in England.

Hendrickson had plucked this unlikely bard from obscurity and had written the definitive account of his life and work, and for good measure had thrown in about thirty pages of notes and a bibliography that induced instant migraine in any reader unlucky enough to come across them. Amazingly, Hendrickson's modest little dodge sparked a small revival in the poet's work, and a commercial publisher expressed interest in bringing out a trade edition minus all the dubious scholarly trappings. The book actually came out and was immediately dispatched to the remainders tables, but this did not dishearten Hendrickson in the least. On the contrary, he was delighted, for the book had accomplished for him everything he had hoped it would—namely, it nailed down his tenure. Hendrickson then figured if he played his cards right, he would never have to contrive a footnote again and could move freely about the area giving little talks to librarians and literary clubs for fifty to a hundred dollars a shot, which was exactly what he was on his way to doing when Henry had run into him.

The two of them fell to reminiscing as they hurried to catch the train and just managed to make the last car before it pulled out. The car was crowded, but Henry spied two empty spaces in a three-across seat and plunked himself down happily, looking forward to a pleasant ride home with good company. Unfortunately, the other occupant of the seat was Casewait.

There was nothing for it but for Henry to engage in some small talk and introduce Hendrickson. Casewait, obviously irritated at being deprived of the luxury of having a whole seat to himself, peered at Hendrickson for a moment, and said, "Don't I know you? You work over at McCann, Ericson?" Hendrickson said no, and admitted to being a college professor. Henry interrupted before Casewait could let Hendrickson know his opinion of college professors and blurted out the fact that Hendrickson had written the definitive biography of such-and-such, the poet.

"Who?" said Casewait.

Henry repeated the poet's name.

"Never heard of him," said Casewait, and gave a contemptuous little snap of his paper.

"Well, " said Hendrickson, apologetically, "I'm afraid he was a very *minor* British poet."

"Don't tell me," said Casewait, putting up his hand, palm forward. "I know everything about him. He was a country vicar and chased after little boys."

"No," said Hendrickson equably, "he was a gentleman farmer and he seems to have preferred adult women for companionship."

Casewait thought that over for a while, then said, "I'll bet he went over to Paris on holidays and had himself whipped."

"No again," said Hendrickson. "He seldom left the country, and from all accounts he was a bit of a physical coward and couldn't stand pain."

"Then he probably liked to lie down and have women with hyphenated names piss on him."

"No," said Hendrickson, refusing to be riled. "He appears to have been ordinary in every way."

"Humph!" snorted Casewait, giving his paper another contemptuous snap. "Doesn't sound like much of a minor British poet to *me*."

Henry thought of this little colloquy as Police Chief Thompson Desplaines leaned back in his chair and said to Henry and Detective Lieutenant Morris, "I really can't say that this fellow Casewait seems much of a villain to *me*."

They were sitting in Desplaines's office in the Municipal Building of the village that, in the absence of any larger municipality, served as the seat of the township. Chief Desplaines had just returned from one of his many trips abroad to attend the various meetings of international law-enforcement agencies to which he belonged. Since he usually paid for these trips himself, the electorate—or, rather, their representatives on the town board, who appointed him—did not object. It could be said of Chief Desplaines that if he were appointed to serve as his country's ambassador to the Court of St. James's, an eventuality that was not entirely out of the question, he was one of the few men who could do so without supplementing his wardrobe. Just now he was wearing a deep-skirted hacking jacket with fawn-colored waistcoat, soft shirt, and checkered ascot. It was difficult to determine whether he had been summoned from stables, kennels, or shooting stand.

"He was married to the Fitzgerald girl, wasn't he?"

"Yes," said Morris. "She was his first wife. Her name was"—he checked his ever ready notebook—"Sylvan." He looked to Henry for corroboration and Henry nodded.

"Ah, yes," said the chief, "Sylvan Fitzgerald." The dreamy expression on his ruddy face indicated that he was summoning up fond memories of summer nights at the country club, the vision of some slip of a girl darting in and out among the potted plants on the patio. "Lovely girl." Then he frowned. "Something wrong there, wasn't there, Lieutenant?"

"Yes, sir," said Morris. "She died in an automobile accident."

"I mean something was *really* wrong, wasn't there?"

"Well, sir," said Morris, "I'm not sure . . . " He motioned with his head toward Henry.

"Oh, yes," said the chief. "I'd forgotten."

"What's all this?" said Henry. "Is it something about Casewait's first wife? I knew her, of course, but we weren't all that close. She kept to herself a great deal."

"Hmm, yes," said the chief. "Well, it's been some time now, so I don't suppose there's any harm in telling you. We have never been satisfied with the verdict of accidental death in that case."

"My God!" exclaimed Henry. "Do you mean to tell me—"

"No, no," said the chief, "nothing like that. What I meant is that we have always felt that it was a case of vehicular suicide."

"Oh," said Henry, and sat back in his chair. Yes, he thought resignedly, it made sense, it had always made sense.

"That's why I was a bit startled when I learned that Casewait was previously married," said Morris. "We had always considered his wife's death as the Fitzgerald file rather than the Casewait file, since she was the native around here. Anyway, you know where it happened, out on old Route 102, where nothing comes by for hours, a perfectly straight stretch of road. She wasn't drunk or even tired, so far as we could tell. Car in perfect condition. She lost control while approaching a handy overpass abutment. We used to call that place Suicide Lane before we finally got the highway department to get rid of that useless overpass."

Chief Desplaines went back to studying the file that was lying open on his desk. Henry and Morris waited respectfully; there was no doubt who was in charge. This was the first time that Henry had met Thompson Desplaines, who was known to his close acquaintances as Tompy. (If Henry had had a name like Thompson, he would have been known as Tommy, but for Desplaines it was Tompy. Henry was not about to try to figure it out.) Previous to this moment, Henry's only acquaintance with the chief was through the society and sports pages of the local newspapers. There was not a charity ball, a cotillion, a sailboat race, a reception for visiting dignitaries, or an opening of a dinner theater that was not graced with his presence.

Henry had always had the impression that the chief was a bubble-headed blueblood who had probably entered police work because of a boyhood affection for the Sherlock Holmes stories. Obviously he had been wrong. The man who sat across the desk from him emanated authority and intelligence. Well, thought Henry, it just goes to show you. Just because a man is rich, handsome, married to a beautiful and talented wife—whose name was Scotty or Ricky or something just as unisexually wholesome—a superb horseman, golfer, tennis player and sailor, and a breeder of championship dogs doesn't necessarily mean that he is stupid, as Henry's mentor, the movies, had taught him and his whole generation.

After a few more moments of contemplation of the folder and its contents, the chief abruptly closed it and pushed it to the far end of his desk. "Well, Lieutenant," he said to Morris, "I would say that's it. You have done a thorough job—you always do—and I guess you can go ahead with the usual procedures. If you need any help from me, if you need me to talk to anyone or just to back you up, I'll be available any time until the middle of next week. Mrs. Desplaines and I are, uh, taking a little trip.

"And now, Mr. Wilnot, as far as *this* goes," he said, motioning to the briefcase filled with bank notes, "we'll have to keep it for the required time, just in case anyone is foolish enough to try to claim it. We'll try to keep it out of the hands of Sheriff Watnell, but if I know him he'll at least demand to be photographed with it. I imagine he's already been informed of its arrival here in the office," he said to Morris.

"Yes," said Morris, "unless Sergeant Greaves has taken the day off." Sergeant Greaves, Henry knew, was the uniformed officer who had first responded to his report of Casewait's death.

"Like any organization that deals with privileged information," the chief explained to Henry, "we have our little security problems. However, no real harm done. If no one claims the money, Mr. Wilnot, it will of course revert to the estate of Mr. Casewait and can be distributed under the terms of the will." My god, thought Henry, Jane and Jeanette are getting richer by the minute! "How's the probate going, by the way?" asked Desplaines.

Somewhat startled, Henry said, "Fine, as far as I know."

"Your man Scanlon's ruffling a few feathers, I understand. He acts rather quickly, and if there's one thing lawyers hereabout resent—or anywhere else, for that matter—it's quick and decisive action."

"Ruffling feathers?" said Henry. "Now what's he done? I didn't mean for him to—"

"Lawyers' business, Mr. Wilnot," he said, waving his hand airily, "leave it to them. Let them fight it out, but scrutinize your bill carefully to make sure you haven't been charged more than the usual amount for personal vendettas. Now, Lieutenant, if you'll check this briefcase with the officer downstairs and give Mr. Wilnot a receipt, we'll take care of any details that have to be gone over."

In the corridor outside of the chief's office, Henry said to Morris, "What was that business about Scanlon? Did that harp come down hard on old Van Dam? If he did, I'll fire him."

"No, no," said Morris, "nothing like that. But his associate, a Miss Nathan, I believe, did swoop down on Roscoe's poor secretary—and made away with your brief or portfolio or whatever they call it. I suspect that Miss Nathan merely told the secretary that she was taking over the probate—following your instructions, of course."

"Certainly," said Henry, "but I didn't think she would resort to strong-arm tactics."

"It was nothing of the sort, Mr. Wilnot," said Morris. "These are just lawyers talking about or with other lawyers. It has nothing to do with personalities or ethics or scruples; only money. Lawyers' talk means nothing but money—that's a lesson the chief taught me when I was just a patrolman." Henry thought that he detected the tone of a man who had spent too much time in courtrooms, which is probably the main occupational hazard of being chief of detectives.

As Henry waited for his receipt—he was relieved to see that the uniformed officer who received the briefcase was neither Harley nor Bierson—he said to Morris, "The chief doesn't seem very concerned about this case. Or is he just leaving the whole thing up to you?"

"On the contrary," said Morris, "he was quite interested in the case, since he knew the first Mrs. Casewait. Anyway, it didn't take him long to figure out what our line of inquiry should be, and it appears to have paid off. We should be able to wrap it all up soon. All we need are replies to a few telexes we've sent."

"*What!*" said Henry, genuinely astonished. "You mean this case is solved?"

"Just about," said Morris unperturbed. "We should know by tomorrow."

Henry relapsed into silence. He was disturbed, and pocketed the receipt for the briefcase distractedly. Telexes meant foreign inquiries.

"By the way," said Morris, "could you ask Mrs. Casewait and Miss Casewait to reserve a bit of time for me tomorrow afternoon, say about two o'clock? I'd like to discuss a few things with them before Mrs. Casewait returns to California. Pure formality," he added.

"Yes, certainly," said Henry, absorbed in thought. Pure formality. He wandered out of the building, a troubled man.

Upon returning home, Henry retired to his study, where he sat lost in thought for a full half hour. He then made a phone call to a local travel agency he had used ever since his children had developed their desire to see the far corners of the world at his expense. He asked a few questions, waited patiently for the answers, hung up, and after consulting the phone directory, phoned Air France in the city. He asked a few more questions and noted the replies. He then rang off, as they say on the continent for some reason; probably something to do with the early days of telephone use. They might still be using the same equipment, for all he knew; he knew he was.

It was with some trepidation that he put in a call to Scanlon.

"Why, hello, Mr. Wilnot," said Miss Nathan cheerfully. "I was just thinking of you."

"Oh?" said Henry, who was more startled than pleased when his call was promptly connected. He was now in a dark and suspicious mood, which naturally meant that everyone around him seemed pleased as punch with life and its jolly course. "In what connection?" he asked sourly.

"Why, your probate, of course," she said. "We have filed the will and perceive no complications whatsoever, apart from any difficulties that may arise due to the manner of death."

"Just what does that mean?" asked Henry.

"Well, I mean the legator was murdered, after all. And if one of the legatees was somehow involved, well, you can see what could happen. But I understand the case is closed and the police are about to press charges against some hired assassin. At least, that's what the sheriff's office has been spreading, with all the means at its disposal."

Which was the last thing Henry wanted to hear.

"I wouldn't be too sure of that," said Henry. "And by the way, you didn't pressure poor Mrs. Hesslin into turning over that will to you, did you? I understand that she's about seventy years old and is holding that office together single-handedly."

"Now don't you worry about that, Mr. Wilnot," scolded Miss Nathan. "We were perfectly within our rights." The ultimate lawyer's defense, thought Henry, summoning up a vision of Miss Nathan storming into ancient law offices and interrupting Mrs. Hesslin at her knitting, flashing her business card like a G-man's badge and ransacking the files.

"And besides," said Miss Nathan, "that office is doing *zilch*, believe me. If we left the will in the hands of those two 'partners' who are supposedly running the place, it would take more than a year to probate. They're off campaigning, according to that poor woman who was left in charge. Campaigning! For what? There aren't any elections for another five months!"

"Probably just keeping their hands in," said Henry, suddenly defensive for the local legal profession, who were nothing if not zealous in perpetuating the democratic process.

"But what do they run *for*?" asked Miss Nathan, showing a little exasperation.

"Anything that requires a decision at the polls," admitted Henry sadly.

"Oh," said Miss Nathan, suddenly understanding and perhaps not wishing to attack her own profession at one of its weakest points.

Could Scanlon be contemplating running for public office? thought Henry. "How's the house sale coming?" he asked, changing the subject. "When does this what's-his-name want to inspect the premises?"

"Mr. Birmingham," she said rather testily. "Didn't you know? He's seen the house already, and they're wild about it."

"When was that?" asked Henry. "Nobody told me anything about it."

"Yesterday," said Miss Nathan. "I guess you were in the city or somewhere, so I just took the liberty of showing them through. And you know what? I think we've got a sale."

"Hmm," said Henry, easily curbing his enthusiasm. "Look, I've just thought of something. Can I really sell this house before the will is probated? Especially considering the manner of the owner's death. I mean, will the court allow it?

"I don't see why not," replied Miss Nathan. "Unless someone contests the will or objects to the sale. Is anyone going to do that?"

"Not that I know of," said Henry. "But it just seems to me that we're getting rid of this property in an awful hurry."

"Well, there's no way we can speed up the means of transferring property, so it will still take quite a while. Look," said Miss Nathan. "I've just thought of something. We could arrange it so that Birmingham could rent the house until the will is probated, with an agreement to buy as soon as it is. That way both of you will have a chance to get to know each other, and if it so happens that you're dissatisfied with each other, then they can refuse to buy or you can refuse to sell. Of course, they'd have a lease, but it would be short term. How does that sound?"

"All right, I guess," said Henry, reminding himself to get a second opinion somewhere, although involving himself with another set of lawyers was not something he relished just now.

"Fine, I'll set it all up," she said. "Anything else?"

"Well, yes. I've been wanting to ask your—I mean, Mr. Scanlon's advice on something else."

"I'm sure I can help you," said Miss Nathan quickly. Henry wondered if she had a second clock to run concurrent with the one that was now running. "And if I can't, I'll simply consult with Mr. Scanlon when he returns from court." The eminent barrister must sleep there, thought Henry. He probably has Chinese food sent in, à la Al Pacino, giving him a chance for an eating scene.

"I don't know exactly how to put this," he said, "but I'm afraid someone I know is about to be charged with the killing of Casewait, and I'd like to do what I can to help, ah, this individual."

"I see," said Miss Nathan, acting not the least surprised. "You say this individual is going to be charged; do you know if he or she actually committed the—ah, let's call it a felony for now."

"I don't know for sure, but everything seems to point to it. I don't see how it could be anyone else."

"But I thought the sheriff was satisfied that it was the work of the Mafia."

"I know, but the local police haven't given that a second thought. They seem to have been following a completely different line of inquiry, and apparently it's paid off. In fact, we're having a get-together tomorrow, and I'm sure the investigating officer is going to treat us to a solution à la Hercule Cluzot or whoever that person is."

"I understand perfectly," said Miss Nathan soothingly. "Now just how do you think you can help this individual?

"By giving advice. You know; not to admit anything, not to say anything until you consult with your attorney, not to identify anything or sign anything. What I need is a strategy."

"Mr. Wilnot," said Miss Nathan indulgently, as though talking to a child—which Henry was, as far as legal knowledge was concerned—"You must know that these days the best tactic is to confess to everything, especially if you're guilty. Blurt it all out, throw in all the details you can think of. Sign a statement if they'll let you."

"But why do that?" asked Henry.

"So that Mr. Scanlon can have the whole thing thrown out of court as tainted evidence obtained while the suspect was under duress. He'd have your friend back on the—I mean, back in the arms of his loved ones in a matter of minutes."

"Hmm," said Henry. Now that she had connected Scanlon with the idea, the whole thing seemed plausible. "I see. Then I don't suppose there'd by any point in having you or Mr. Scanlon there when the charges are made?"

"Good Lord, no!" said Miss Nathan. "That's the worst thing you could do. On the other hand, if you could have some legal representatives from the other side present, that would be ideal. We could charge intimidation, veiled threat, coercion—the possibilities are practically endless. I don't suppose you could get the county prosecutor to drop by, could you?" She giggled girlishly.

So that's what it is, thought Henry, a game they play with each other, for enormous fees paid by their luckless clients. His silence must have communicated his displeasure to Miss Nathan.

"I'm sorry, Mr. Wilnot," she said. "I didn't mean to sound frivolous, but there's quite a bit of truth in all of what I said. And if you're sure of your friend's innocence, or lack of criminal intent, or just plain misfortune, then the best thing is to do nothing and hear the investigating officer out."

"Hmm," said Henry, not the least bit reassured.

"Look, Mr. Wilnot," said Miss Nathan, "I don't know if you are thinking of retaining counsel for yourself or for someone else— It's not for *you*, is it, by the way? I mean *you* didn't shoot Casewait did you?"

"Well, *I* know I didn't, anyway," said Henry, "but I don't know if anybody else does." He saw no need to tell her that he was sitting on a quarter of a million dollars of laundered Mafia money.

"Good," said Miss Nathan. "Then I tell you what. Why don't you let us start preparing the preliminaries for a defense now, while we have the jump on the district attorney's office. There are all sorts of things we could do before sources of information are closed down, if you know what I mean. We have all sorts of people who can begin investigating clues or alibis or whatever . . . "

I'll bet you have, thought Henry, but he was intrigued.

". . . and if we come up with anything that would help, we'd turn it over to you even if you or your friend decided to retain other counsel."

Fat chance, thought Henry. He felt that he was now so far in the clutches of Scanlon and his familiar, the feline Miss Scanlon, that he risked losing his soul if he crossed them.

"There's one other thing, of course," purred Miss Nathan.

"Oh, what's that?" asked Henry with the sinking feeling that he knew what it was.

"The name of your friend. And the reasons for your suspicions."

"Must I?" pleaded Henry.

"Mr. Wilnot," said Miss Nathan, "if it's confidentiality you're worried about, I should remind you that I Am a Lawyer."

Under ordinary circumstances such a statement, coming from anyone, man or woman, would have sent Henry searching for the nearest exit, but he had to admit that she had him cold.

"All right," said Henry, relieved in spite of himself. Let somebody else tussle with this problem. He told her the name of the person who had shot Casewait.

There was a moment of silence on the line. Miss Nathan said, "Are you sure?"

"I don't see how it could be anyone else," said Henry.

"I see," said Miss Nathan. Another silence. Finally, "Could you give me what you have, please?"

Henry did.

16

FOR HENRY, ONE of the pleasures in reading detective fiction was the sheer predictability of the proceedings. He awaited the set pieces and the obligatory scenes with the same anticipation he had awaited, as a child, the comic shticks of his favorite radio comedians. Week after week Red Skelton's Mean Wittle Kid had said, "I dood it!" Fibber McGee had opened his closet, and Jack Benny had descended into his vault leaving the preadolescent Henry weak with laughter and shaking his head in wonderment of it all. What gifts!

Now, older and presumably wiser, in book after book Henry no less eagerly awaited the discovery of the body, the introduction of the sleuth, the false lead, the death of the prime suspect, the sleuth's nagging memory of something he had heard or seen somewhere, sometime. But of all these ritualistic shenanigans, none was dearer to Henry's heart than the confrontation between the detective—be he or she a professional law officer, amateur sleuth, savant, or, in certain recherché works, witty deviant—and the suspects, each of whom was as guilty as sin so far as Henry could discern. The fun, of course, was in the variations rung on the familiar tune, never forgetting for a moment that the unraveling and the sorting out was all.

Henry usually tried to avoid such scenes in his own fiction, not because he felt that he wasn't up to the high standards that had been set from the days of Conan Doyle, but just that his private eyes were not up to stretches of dialogue lasting more than half a page. If his fictional Clagen, for instance, ever assembled a group of suspects in one room, the cowardly wretch who had done it would, after taking one look at

Clagen's clouded visage and hairy paws, give a little whimper and break for the door, or in some cases the window, provoking Clagen to a flying tackle and bone-crushing punch-out.

The group assembled in the living room of Casewait's house—the setting for the forthcoming scene had been Morris's choice—resembled more a gathering of strangers in an airport lounge than the dramatis personae in a tea cozy thriller. Jeanette, clad in a fetching traveling outfit consisting of what looked to Henry like pajamas made of some stout material, sat nervously rummaging through her huge handbag as though checking for her boarding pass. Jane, wearing her usual pants suit, sat quietly in a wing chair, hands folded demurely in her lap and legs crossed at the ankles, with the serene look of the perpetual traveler eternally between stops. Erica, in a tweed skirt, sweater and blouse, stout shoes, and stockings so sensible that they looked as though they were woven with string, looked to be exactly what she was—a Teuton bent on getting to where she intended going. In the present case, this happened to be her native Germany, to which she had renewed her resolve to return, as she had explained to Henry several times since the contretemps with Zawwada, the sound amplifier, and the hounds of hell.

Erica had expressed surprise at being invited to Morris's little theatrical and complained bitterly that it would interfere with her appointments with travel agent, hairdresser, various department store clerks, and, for all Henry knew, her tobacconist, vintner, and butcher. Once set in motion, she was the familiar Deutscher juggernaut, crashing through everything in her way until she came to rest in the haven of her mother's apartment outside Stuttgart. Here she would put down her packages, distribute gifts to whatever relatives and family retainers were still alive, and, after stuffing herself with all manner of cold meats and starches, begin the serious business of being bored to distraction. In a week or two Henry would be called to fetch her, either from Germany itself or from one of the nearby airports catering to international flights—with any luck from the latter, as far as Henry was concerned.

Now, among these transients, he already felt like the useless stay-at-home, good for nothing but checking or collecting bags, inquiring dates of arrival or departure, pointing out rest rooms, and trying desperately not to succumb to the temptation of the airport bar. He sat down in a club chair and stared at Casewait's magazine rack as though it were a newsstand.

Detective Lieutenant Morris, who had donned a three-piece suit complete with watch fob for the occasion, had greeted them at the door after they had filed across from Henry's after a late breakfast. He introduced them to his amanuensis, the taciturn and mysterious Harrison, and chatted easily with the women as they disposed themselves among the furniture in the living room, which Henry noted was polished, vacuumed, waxed, and to judge by the appearance of one or two pieces, refinished. No refreshments were offered, which Henry considered a breach of etiquette: he seemed to recall that tea or coffee used to be poured out by the gallons at such affairs staged by his favorite authors. In this area, thought Henry, there was much to be said for the American way of doing things. He could have used a stiff drink.

"Well," said Morris, assuming his stance at the focal center of the room in front of a double window overlooking a wall of greenery, "shall we get started?" He smiled to himself and actually rubbed his hands together. Henry groaned inwardly. He was beginning to lose confidence in his favorite detective lieutenant already. No mere mortal cop could carry this sort of thing off. It would take at least a year at the Royal Academy of Dramatic Art and a couple of seasons in repertory before one could even begin to assay the role. "I thought it would be a good idea if we all got together before we went our separate ways," said Morris, nodding gallantly to Jeanette, "in case there was any misunderstanding about our several—how shall I put it?—*responsibilities* concerning the death of Mr. Casewait. I'm sure that you can appreciate that in a matter such as this the police must consider anyone connected with the deceased a suspect. This means, of course, that we have had to delve rather deeply into your recent movements, and in some cases, unfortunately, into your past."

Henry noticed that a vague uneasiness had crept over the gathering, and he felt that he may have been its progenitor. "Everyone?" he asked.

"Yes," said Morris. "Everyone."

They all looked at Erica, who was staring at her folded hands and slowly turning beet red. The curse of the northern European complexion, thought Henry, not unkindly.

"But what about all that has happened to Henry?" protested Jeanette. "I thought the sheriff said that the case was closed as far as he was concerned?"

"Oh, yes," said Morris, "that aspect of the case is closed, but there still remains the problem of your late husband's murder."

"But I thought that was all part of it," persisted Jeanette. "That Joe was killed by those horrible mobsters who were using him for something or other. It was in the papers."

"I know," said Morris, "but oftentimes what appears in the papers has no connection with what is actually going on. In this case, the sheriff's office was pursuing one line of investigation and we, the local police, another."

Henry wasn't listening. He was staring at his wife, whose face was still a startling red. She was obviously in an agony of embarrassment—or guilt. Henry had known for some time, of course—Casewait had not been the most discreet of adulterers—but he had never been able to figure out just when it was that his neighbor had insinuated himself into the deepest recesses of his family, so to speak.

In his youth, Henry had studied comparative literature,

and now the whole rich panoply of cuckoldry as depicted by great authors from Chaucer to Machado seemed to parade before his inner eye. No wonder they were so partial to the subject, he thought; giants they had to be to tackle it! He himself was beginning to think it was the mightiest theme known to man.

Erica glanced at him, and she knew that he knew. Damn! thought Henry. This was going to take some sorting out. How deeply had Erica been involved with Casewait, never mind when and how? Did it in any way implicate her in his shooting? Where had she been on the night in question? In bed, so far as Henry knew. And where had he been? Sitting in his den musing over some delicious caper, naturally. That was the trouble with him and all other artists, he decided, so caught up in themselves and their work that they didn't notice what was going on right under their noses.

Whenever he was depressed or feeling sorry for himself, Henry thought of himself as an artist, whereas when he was in tip-top shape, at the top of his form, he considered himself a simple craftsman, an honest scribbler who left all the beauty, profundity, and grace to the deep-dish boys. Now, in his depression, he realized that it was not the artistic natures who did all the womanizing, despite their reputation in the popular mind; no, not by a long shot. It was the hotshot politicians, the businessmen, lawyers, and surgeons who were so busy that they found no trouble in squeezing an illicit affair or two into their full schedules. Those with sensitive natures like himself, however, were too preoccupied with their rich inner lives, too involved in spinning whole worlds out of airy nothingness to remember to take the time to deflower their students, screw their secretaries, or seduce their neighbors' wives.

These bitter musings had prevented Henry from giving his attention to Detective Lieutenant Morris's preamble, which under normal circumstances he would have listened to attentively in hopes of picking up some tips or some little bit of business that he could insert into one of Clagen's adventures.

"Now," Lieutenant Morris was saying, "I won't bother you with the preliminaries of the case. Just let me say that we have determined that this was a simple unpremeditated murder, probably committed in a fit of passion or rage, or even temporary insanity, which accounts for most of your ordinary homicides, particularly among family members or close acquaintances."

Henry glanced around the room. None of the three women seemed to realize what the lieutenant was leading up to—or else they were remarkably good actresses, the best among them his wife, he now realized.

"I know what you're going to say," said Morris, making the stop sign with his hand, as if to halt the flood of objections that were streaming his way. No one in the room seemed disposed to make any, so the lieutenant continued.

"What of the possibility of robbery? you may ask. Or could it have been suicide? Or an accident: one of those gun-cleaning incidents that regularly carry away a good portion of our citizenry."

My God! thought Henry, he's rehearsed this. The mysterious Harrison, who had ceased taking notes and was now staring raptly at his boss, seemed more prompter than amanuensis.

"Well," persevered the lieutenant in the face of his audience's nonexistent objections, "I can assure you that we have considered every possibility, and that every one of them, when it was warranted, was investigated. The possibility of armed robbery, for example, was rejected after the most routine police work at the low—at the most basic level: the physical evidence itself." Morris must have had Harley and Bierson in mind there, thought Henry. "There was no sign of forced entry, no sign of violence whatsoever, and I can assure you also that armed robbers do not clean up after their work. Nothing was disturbed. In fact, the only physical marks not of an ordinary nature were some tire marks on the grass border a short distance from the front of the house, and to tell you the truth, the only reason those were remarked and investigated was because of Mr. Wilnot's statement that he heard a car start and leave in some haste shortly before he discovered the body."

Henry pondered this observation for a moment. He now realized that he himself was the key to this whole affair. He was the only witness to events, slight as they were, just before and after the finding of the body. It was he who had been coshed on an unannounced and devious trip to the city allegedly to investigate Casewait's office furniture; it was he who had become involved in Zawwada's attempts to recover Casewait's laundry; it was he who had found and discovered the use of the key to Casewait's storage box. It was a chain of events that must have seemed highly unlikely to be coincidence. But beyond that, nothing. Could it be that the police had constructed a case against him? He felt a surge of optimism. *He* knew he hadn't shot Casewait, but if they thought he had, it meant that they didn't suspect who he knew did it. Wonderful! Press on Morris. Do your damnedest.

"As to the possibility of suicide or accident," continued Morris, there is simply no getting around the fact that the weapon that caused the wound that eventually was responsible for the death of Mr. Casewait has disappeared. And without that there is nothing left but the inescapable conclusion that the wound was caused by a third party. And that third party was . . ." Here he paused and allowed himself a ruminative smile. "Someone with a gun."

His little joke, while not exactly greeted with groans, fell flat. Besides its being cribbed from Dashiell Hammett, thought Henry, it was remarkably insensitive. After all, Morris's audience for his feeble one-liners consisted of the dead man's wife, daughter, erstwhile mistress, and former best friend. Henry shifted in his chair and tried to convey his disapproval by clearing his throat and grumbling after the manner of Nigel Bruce.

"Sorry," said Morris, "I'm afraid that wasn't very funny. Well, then, to get down to business, what we have here is a simple homicide, probably committed on the spur of the moment and then hastily covered up by the removal of the evidence and the construction of an alibi or alibis. Alibis, by the way"—here he paused again, this time to let his words sink in—"that are full of holes."

To say that Morris's audience was rapt would be an understatement. This was the lieutenant's first indication that he considered one of them to be the murderer—who else did he have alibis from?—and the implication was not lost on any of them. Even Henry began to run over in his mind every movement and statement he had made immediately before and after the day involved. He glanced at his fellow auditors: Jeanette and Jane were staring at Morris, waiting for elucidation; Erica alone showed any emotion other than anxiety. She seemed flustered and avoided Henry's eyes.

"Perhaps," continued Morris, "it might be clearer as to what we're up to if you look at things from our—the police's that is—point of view. We are called here to examine a body that has been shot and submerged in a swimming pool. Period. That's all we know. We gather all the information from the first person on the scene, the one who reported finding the body." He bowed in the direction of Henry, who nodded back, modestly.

"He, unfortunately for him, becomes our first suspect. Now," he said, holding up his hand in the familiar stop signal, "I know what you're thinking: 'How like the police, and no wonder everybody hesitates to even report a crime, let alone get involved in giving evidence or supporting the investigators.' But that's the way it is. We simply have to start somewhere, so we start with the first person we have at hand who is in any way involved in the crime. And that was Mr.

Wilnot here." He held his hand out, palm up, in Henry's direction: Ta-dah.

"We are not overstaffed," Morris went on, "so we like to keep the men we have at our disposal busy at the scene of the crime. At this point in our investigation, the only person—besides the victim, of course—they could busy themselves with was Mr. Wilnot. As a case wears on, naturally, other persona become worthy of their busyness, and the initial concentration on one person becomes less intense, but by that time we have just about all we need to know about the person who reported the crime."

By this time Henry had slid down in his chair and was peering over his church-steepled fingers like a trapped animal. If they had learned even half the things that regularly caused him to pull the pillow over his head at night, he was a gone goose, at least in this town, where just about anything went just so long as it also went undiscovered and undisclosed.

"I wouldn't trouble you with any of the details of Mr. Wilnot's file even if I could, but I would like to examine his alibi." Morris turned to Henry and smiled almost fondly at him. "It is very easily examined, for you see, the truth is that Mr. Wilnot does not have an alibi."

"Oh, come on, now," said Jeanette.

"Really!" said Erica.

Jane said nothing but continued to look at her hands folded demurely in her lap.

"Yes, I know," said Morris, who seemed to be enjoying himself. "And I agree with you. Personally I never thought that Mr. Wilnot had anything to do with the shooting of Mr. Casewait, but I could not ignore the fact that he did not have an alibi that could be checked. And therefore he became a suspect."

"But I told you all my movements, and my wife confirmed them," Henry protested weakly.

"Yes," said Morris, "on the day before the murder you

worked in your studio until a little after five o'clock, had cocktails and chatted with your wife until you both dined at seven thirty. You then read awhile, listened to a concert on the radio, and then at eleven o'clock joined your wife in the television room to watch the news, followed by Johnny Carson, who you watched until about twelve, when your wife departed for bed. You stayed up a bit longer because Johnny had put out a teaser to the effect that the Mighty Carson Art Players would be doing a sketch later on, but you soon became drowsy and decided to call it a night, Mighty Carson Art Players or no," Morris paused and looked at Henry. "Those were your exact words."

Henry slumped further into his seat and let his arms fall away from him, his palms turned upward, as if to say, Take me, I'm guilty. "I've never pretended to any style," he said. "Either in my life or work."

"You awoke at your usual time, which is six o'clock, and went through your usual morning routine until a quarter after seven or thereabouts, when you left by your back door to go to your work shed. You noticed Mr. Casewait leaving his house and walking with some difficulty toward his swimming pool. You also heard a car door slam and an engine start and roar away from the road in front of your house. When you arrived at your work shed you observed the body of Mr. Casewait floating in his . . ." Morris frowned at his notes, which probably contained Henry's description of the loathed pool—"pestilential sinkhole," it might have been. "In his swimming pool," he finished. "You then somehow retrieved the body from the water—you're still unclear as to how you managed this?" he asked Henry, who nodded affirmatively.

"Anyway, having beach—having retrieved the body, you returned to your home and awoke your wife and phoned the police. This was approximately seven forty. Is that true?"

"By your log it probably is," said Henry, "but it took me at least five minutes to get through to the station. *That* early in the morning," he added peevishly.

"One of our busiest times," said Morris, unperturbed. "Commuters are thronging the highways and running into and over one another, domestic disputes are coming to a head at the breakfast table, bathroom injuries are being reported—"

"All right, all right," muttered Henry.

"Now, Mr. Wilnot, I will ask you to try to reconstruct exactly what you did between the time you hung up the phone and the time the first police arrived on the scene."

"What on earth for?" said Henry. "I've told you that nothing happened. My wife came downstairs and I told her what had happened, and then I returned to Casewait's pool and waited over the body until the police arrived, like a faithful dog."

"What did you say, exactly, to your wife?"

"I told her that Casewait had been shot. I believe my exact words were, 'Casewait has been shot.' "

"Hmm," said Morris.

"Lieutenant," said Henry, "isn't this what the legal profession calls a fishing expedition?"

Morris smiled. "I suppose you're right, but I just wanted to make sure that you never had any suspicion that anyone else was in Casewait's house."

"The thought occurred to me much later that, of course, there had to be another person in the house."

"Or two," said Morris.

"*What*?" said Henry. "You mean that there were two people involved in Casewait's death?" He thought about this for a moment. "Well, I guess you could be right. Two people could have been in that car that took off from in front of the house—but wait a minute. Wouldn't that reinforce the sheriff's idea that Casewait was done in by the mob?" Hemingway's "The Killers" came to his mind.

"No, not necessarily. The two people could have been unawarc of each other's presence."

"I don't get it," said Henry.

"Oh, it's not too difficult," said Morris. "But why don't we ask one of the persons who was there?"

He turned to Jane and said, "What did you do after you saw your father on the floor with a bullet wound, Miss Casewait?"

Jane continued to stare at her folded hands. "I did what I always do when I'm confused or upset," she said quietly.

"And what was that, Miss Casewait?"

"I cleaned the house."

17

"WAIT, JANE!" SHOUTED Henry, leaping to his feet. All of the advice Miss Nathan had given him went right out of the window. "Don't say a thing! He can't get anything out of you until he reads you your rights or something. Just keep quiet and I'll have a lawyer here in no time."

"Please, Mr. Wilnot," said Morris, indulgently. He seemed so satisfied with himself and the little dramatic coup he had just brought off that he remained unruffled at Henry's outburst. "There's no need for a lawyer or for formal charges. No one's accusing Miss Casewait of anything. I'm just curious as to what happened in this house that night, that's all."

Shades of *In Cold Blood*, thought Henry, unkindly. He looked at Jane, who was still sitting calmly with her hands folded in her lap and her legs crossed at the ankles. It was obvious to him that she wasn't very much interested in her own defense. He fell back into his chair grumbling, sounding more like Nigel Bruce than ever.

"Now, Miss Casewait," said Morris, speaking quietly and with much deference to the pitifully vulnerable figure in the wing chair. "Where were you when your father was shot?"

"I was in my old bedroom, sleeping."

"And how did you come to be there?"

"I had arrived that day on the Concorde from Paris. I think we landed about eight forty-five or nine o'clock. We'd left Paris at eleven, so I was suffering from jet lag, or maybe it was just fatigue, since I'd flown into Paris from Geneva that morning. I rented a car at the airport and drove out here. I believe I arrived at about ten thirty, or maybe it was eleven. I can't be sure about anything."

"I understand," said Morris sympathetically. "Where did you park your car, the one you rented?"

"On the grass just off the road between our house and Mr. Wilnot's house, sort of under that overgrown privet out there." Henry winced. He'd have to get that damn thing properly trimmed one of these days. If nothing else, this investigation was turning up more and more of his deficiencies as a homeowner.

"Why didn't you park in the driveway?"

"My father's station wagon was parked there. It takes up quite a bit of room." Morris glanced at Harrison, who nodded in some sort of agreement.

"Why did you come here, Miss Casewait? Back to this country, I mean?"

"My father had been calling me for weeks. He said he needed me for a very important reason, actually two very important reasons. He said he was trying to effect a reconciliation with Jeanette and he needed me to convince her that it would work. He also had a very important errand for me to perform."

"Did he tell you what the errand was?"

"No, he just said that it was extremely important and could affect our future lives together."

"Miss Casewait," said Morris, "during our first interview you said that you were attending a symposium or some sort of meeting in Paris, and even though you misled us as to the time of your arrivals and departures, I assume that this meeting was a real one and that your presence was required or expected there."

"Yes."

"Now, why did you interrupt your plans so suddenly to return home?"

"When I arrived at my hotel there was an urgent message from my father to call him at once. I put through the call, and he practically demanded that I return home immediately. He said that if I didn't he couldn't answer for the consequences.

He implied that Jeanette was in danger, and that only I could help her."

"Did you have any idea what the danger could be?"

"No, but I had the idea that she was in danger from my father more than from anything else."

"Oh?" said Morris. "Why was that?"

Jane shrugged. "I don't know. He just sounded threatening, that's all."

That bastard! thought Henry. He could well imagine Casewait virtually blackmailing his own daughter with threats against her stepmother.

"How did your father know where you were staying in Paris?"

"I told him when he called me the week before in Lausanne."

"I see. Did anyone else know you would be there?"

"No."

Morris seemed to be tiring from standing for so long, so he went into the dining room and pulled a chair from the table, bringing it into the living room, where he twirled it around with a deft movement and straddled it, leaning his forearms on the back. Henry understood that detectives liked to sit this way to prevent people they had detained for questioning from kicking them in the balls—an almost irresistible temptation for the suspects, as he was finding out.

"Where did you find your father when you came downstairs?" asked Morris, his private parts now covered.

"There," she said, pointing to the area between the dining room and the kitchen.

"Did you believe he was dead?"

"Yes. I could see the wound. There was hardly any blood, but he was very still, and he just looked dead to me."

"And then you proceeded to clean the house."

"Yes. That doesn't sound very logical, but I'm afraid I was in slight shock, plus being worn out from all the flying time I'd put in the last few days."

"Did you hear the shot that wounded your father?"

"No."

"What brought you downstairs, then?"

"I was thirsty. I mean incredibly thirsty. It had awakened me."

"Couldn't you have gotten a drink of water from the bathroom?"

"Yes, I suppose so, but I just wasn't thinking properly."

It seemed to Henry that Morris wasn't buying her story, at least not all of it. "Look, Lieutenant," he said, "isn't this being rather relentless? This poor girl has been through a great deal in the past week. Couldn't you let up for a while?"

"Yes, of course," said Morris. "I'm sorry, Miss Casewait, but perhaps you'll let me summarize what we believe was the sequence of events, and if I'm wrong you can interrupt me: You left Lausanne for Paris and arrived without incident on the day before your father was killed. You checked into your hotel and left almost immediately for Charles de Gaulle Airport, leaving your luggage at the hotel and carrying an overnight bag. You took the eleven o'clock Concorde and arrived here at eight forty-five or thereabouts. You rented a car and arrived at your father's house about ten thirty and shortly thereafter went to bed. You awoke about four o'clock and found your father lying apparently dead on the floor between the dining room and the kitchen. You then cleaned the house, collected your overnight bag, and left the house at exactly seven twenty, which gave you plenty of time to drive to the airport and catch the one o'clock Concorde back to Paris. You arrived at Charles de Gaulle at about ten forty-five their time, four forty-five ours. You either called or returned to your hotel to learn of Mr. Wilnot's call and message to call back."

Jane listened to all of this passively, giving no visible sign of either denying or agreeing with anything Morris was saying.

"Now, Miss Casewait," said Morris gently, "I have only a

few more questions to ask you. First, all of your transactions—the purchase of airline tickets and the car rental—were made in cash, so far as we can tell. Where did you get all the money?"

"My father wired a great deal of cash to me, which I picked up at Charles de Gaulle. And when I arrived here, the first thing he did was thrust a wad of bills at me. I think he was trying to impress me. 'This is what it's all about, babe,' he said, or something like that. I think he had been drinking. Anyway, I forgot all about the bills until I got to the airport for the return trip. And then I just used them, I guess."

"Second, Miss Casewait, you said that when you arrived here your father's station wagon was in the driveway. Was it there when you left?"

"No."

"I see," said Morris. "And now, finally, why didn't you tell us of all this, since you must have known that your movements could be traced?"

"I just never thought you'd even consider that I was here, that's all."

"But why didn't you want us to know?"

"I don't know," she said more weakly than ever.

Morris sighed and pushed himself up from his chair. He spun the chair around by the back and sat down again facing them in the conventional manner. "Well," he said, "that clears things up considerably; wouldn't you say so, Mr. Wilnot?"

"Oh, definitely," said Henry, "except for one little point. Who shot Casewait?"

"Why, the other person who was in the house at the time," said Morris.

Oh, Christ! thought Henry. He sat up straight in his chair and looked frantically at Erica. Had she crept across the lawn while he was asleep and done Casewait in over some illicit lovers' quarrel? Erica, however, was not reddening guiltily, but was looking horrifiedly at Morris. Henry looked back at

Morris, and then leaned back in his chair and groaned quietly to himself.

Morris was looking straight at Jeanette.

18

"HE WAS BLACKMAILING me," said Jeanette tensely. "I flew in from Los Angeles to try to reason with him, but he wouldn't listen. I didn't know Jane was in the house. I'd noticed the car parked in front, but I thought it was probably Henry's or one of his kids'."

"How was he blackmailing you, Mrs. Casewait?" asked Morris.

"It goes back a long way," she said. Sighing resignedly, she leaned back in her chair, all tension gone. "I might as well tell you everything. All of you."

Henry felt like excusing himself. If there was one thing he didn't want to hear it was the confession of a good friend who had been so intimately acquainted with Casewait that she had left herself open to blackmail. Putting the fingers of one hand over his eyes, he leaned forward in his chair and stared at the portion of rug between his feet. He had no doubt this was going to be painful.

"When I first met Joe, he was still at Baines and Barlowe. In fact, he was the hottest thing there, virtually running his own personal show. I was operating my own talent agency then, and I met him in the normal course of business. That is, I made an appointment with him to show him some portfolios of my girls, and he asked me out to lunch. And then it just went on from there, the way those things usually do.

"The only trouble was, he wanted my girls to do more than just model for ads or appear in commercials. He was involved with many restaurant and entertainment accounts then, and you can guess what that means. Anyway, whenever some big accounts came in from out of town, Joe would lay on entertainment for them, which included girls. I'm sorry to say that I supplied them. I was just starting out on my own and I was desperate to succeed, and anyway the girls didn't seem to mind; in fact, most of them seemed to enjoy it and looked forward to the assignments. There were a few junkets to Florida, and weekend parties at some big lodge in the Adirondacks that one of Joe's restaurant people ran. But I never liked any of it, and one of the conditions I made when Joe asked me to marry him after his wife died was that I never had to do anything like that again.

"Joe lived up to his end of the bargain with a vengeance. He virtually stranded me out here, while he went about his old ways in the city. Not that I didn't like it out here," she said, looking at Henry and Erica. "Actually, after a while I began to prefer it to my old way of life. Erica, you know that. I even joined the PTA.

"Anyway, our marriage went progressively downhill, and if it hadn't been for Jane here I would have left him years before I did. When I finally did leave, I went home to Los Angeles and was given this incredible chance to start all over again. I got my old job back with the Hollywood branch of an agency I'd worked for in the city and gradually built up a fine stable—and I mean that almost literally," she said, laughing tearfully, "since I handle a lot of animal acts. Anyway, I was finally settling down into what I felt would be my life's work. And to top everything off, my boss was just getting over a messy divorce, and we took to each other like two actors at a stockbrokers' party."

She sniffed and took a handkerchief out of her enormous bag and blew her nose daintily. She had the complete and rapturous attention of everyone in the room, including Henry, who had gradually uncovered his eyes and was now sitting upright, drinking in every word. It was a hell of a story, and Jeanette was telling it well. Henry felt that it could go directly, untouched and unedited, into one of those lugubrious television dramas Erica watched every afternoon.

"I really thought my life had turned into the most splendid adventure possible," continued Jeanette, "and then, out of the blue, I got a call from Joe, who said that he wanted us to start all over again. He said he'd made some sort of a big killing and he was going to live in Europe with Jane and me. We were all going to make a new start in France or Switzerland or maybe even one of the Greek or Spanish islands. He was talking crazier than usual, and I thought he must be drunk or on something, so I just hung up on him.

"Well, that must have done it, because he started calling me every day and night, and once even got through to me at my office. He started threatening me that if I didn't come back to him he'd expose me to my boss, tell him about what I used to do for him before we were married. He didn't know that Barney—that's my boss—and I were going together, because that would have sent him right over the edge. Maybe he did know, and was already over the edge; I don't know. When he threatened to go to the Association of Independent Producers and expose me, I panicked. The next day I had lunch with Barney and then made up some story that I had to see some animal act clients out in the Valley; then I took the three fifteen flight and arrived here around eleven twenty. I was so upset that I took a cab from the airport and got here about twelve thirty.

"I had no idea that Jane was in the house. Joe had been drinking, of course, and was bragging about this big deal he had made, which had set him up for life. He said that if I didn't believe him I could call Jane. He even gave me her number in Paris! Why he pretended that she was still in Europe I'll never know. Maybe he thought he'd surprise me by going upstairs and bringing her down. Who knows what was going through that excuse for a mind. Did I ever tell you that he drove his first wife to suicide? I'm sorry, Jane, but I'm sure he did, just as sure as I am that he was willing to ruin me if I didn't come back to him.

"Then he started muttering something about having enemies and how he had to get away soon. He took a gun out of that drawer over there and showed it to me, probably to prove that he was still his old macho self and could take care of anybody who came up against him.

"God, he was hateful! He said that this was my last chance, and was I going to go with him. I said no, and he said all right, he was going to call my boss. I knew that Barney was working late that night, and what with the time difference he might conceivably still be at the office. When Joe started dialing the phone, I became absolutely frantic, and I guess I picked up the gun and shot him.

"He fell down and I didn't know whether he was dead or alive. I just knew that I had to get out of this house. I ran out the front door and actually ran in circles on the front lawn. I even considered going over to your house, Henry, but thank God I got control of myself before doing that. I'm telling you, I was so frantic and confused and frightened that I didn't know what to do or where to go. Then I remembered that I still had keys to the station wagon on my key ring, so I just got in and drove away. By the time I settled down and got control of myself, I was already halfway to the airport, so I just kept on going. I caught the six forty-five flight and was back in Los Angeles by eleven twenty. I live just a few minutes from the airport, so I was home by the time your men called, Lieutenant."

"Hmm, yes," said Morris. "Tell me, Mrs. Casewait, did you keep the gun, by any chance?"

"No, I threw it out of the window on some parkway between here and the airport. Sorry. I hope it doesn't fall into the wrong hands."

Morris did not say anything to that, but again consulted his notebook. Henry could guess what he was thinking: All we need around here is another unregistered gun, especially if it's found on the side of the road by a hitchhiker or a bunch of kids.

Morris looked up from his notebook and said, "You're a travel agent, aren't you, Mrs. Casewait?"

"Why yes, I have been for years; I have to arrange a lot of travel for my clients. Why do you ask?"

"I just wondered how you could pop in and out of airports and always get a flight."

"Yes, I have a card that makes it very easy, dammit!"

It was an odd note to end on, but apparently Morris had decided that this most lamentable comedy *era finito*. "Well," he said, slapping his knees and rising briskly from his chair, "that about does it, I guess. We can assume that Mr. Casewait regained consciousness just as Miss Casewait left the house, and then, in his confused—to say the least—state of mind, attempted to retrieve the key that Mr. Wilnot so cleverly put his hands on the next day. He must have fallen or stumbled when he reached the platform of his pool and fell into the water. The cause of death, by the way, Mrs. Casewait, was drowning. There was water in his lungs, indicating that he was still alive when he fell into the water."

"Just what does that mean?" asked Henry. "I mean, what will Jeanette be charged with?"

"I don't know," said Morris. "I explained to you, Mr. Wilnot, that I am not a lawyer. I was merely interested in finding out what went on in this house. What the county prosecutor's office will make of it, I have no idea. I suggest, however, that Mrs. Casewait and her attorney appear at police headquarters tomorrow morning at ten o'clock. You can make a formal statement then."

Henry couldn't believe his ears. Was this cop going to walk away from a collar? He thought that that was what these guys lived for. "Book 'em, Danno," that stony-faced TV cop used to say, and then smirk shamelessly at the camera. Detective Lieutenant Morris, however, was apparently having none of that. Either he was a hopeless romantic who couldn't bring himself to charge a good-looking woman, or he was about to retire with all the graft he had collected over the years.

"I'll be there, Lieutenant," said Jeanette with relief and gratitude.

All the people in the room had risen from their chairs and were standing around wondering what to do next. It was a situation in which Henry seemed regularly to have found himself for much of his adult life, like one of those faculty-parent meetings he had been attending for over twenty years, from his children's kindergarten days through the university. He felt that at any moment he was going to be asked to write out a whopping big check. As in the past when confronted with such an eventuality he began edging toward the door, signaling to Erica that he was leaving things in her hands.

"Oh, Mr. Wilnot," said Lieutenant Morris, heading him off as skillfully as any alumni fund-raiser. "Could I see you for a minute?"

"Of course," said Henry, abandoning all hope. "Hey, but listen, how 'bout a drink or something first? I'm sure we could all use one. Hey, everybody," he said to the women and the saturnine Harrison, "how about some refreshments? I'm sure we can scare something up here, or, better yet, let's go over to our house. We can fix something for all of us."

They all agreed with a little flutter of anticipation and began grabbing for handbags, gloves, keys, pads, pencils, and anything else they could lay their hands on in order to indicate the alacrity and joy with which they responded to the prospect of visiting the humble house next door. Henry had the feeling that if he had suggested that they all go over to the Unitarian minister's house and look at the slides of that worthy's trip to Hawaii they would have flung themselves out the door in their excitement.

"You go ahead, Erica," he said to their retreating backs. "I'll be over in a few minutes."

He and Morris stood watching them through a window as they hustled across the lawn. Not for them any curiosity as to the solution of the slightly bizarre case they had been involved in. Lemme outta here! would more accurately describe their reaction to Lieutenant Morris's cleverly planned denouement.

"I can see that the principals in this case are not too concerned about the subtleties of its solution," said Morris.

"Sherlock Holmes could not have put it better," said Henry. "But never mind, Lieutenant, I just think they're so relieved that it's over and no one has been ruined or even damaged, that they've forgotten for the moment that there was any mystery involved at all. In fact, *they* knew all along what had happened—or at least a good part of it."

"That's truc," said Morris, turning from the window and walking back into the living room, where Harrison was quietly packing up his notes. Morris settled himself into an easy chair and motioned for Henry to do the same. They both stared into the middle distance until Harrison had made his departure. Henry wished that he had brought along one of his pipes so that he could have poked at it ruminatively.

"You know what bothered me most about Mrs. Casewait's story?" said Morris suddenly.

Henry sat up, startled. "You mean you didn't believe it?" he asked.

"Oh, I believed it. Or at least, most of it. No, I was thinking of what she said about dashing out of the house and running in circles on the lawn. I never even noticed it, or even gave orders to have the area cordoned off so that we could go over it. I was so sure that everything about this case was confined to what happened inside the house that I neglected the outside entirely."

"Well, good Lord, what good would it have done?" said Henry. "By the time you got here, that sergeant—what was his name, that spy of Big Sam's?"

"Greaves."

"Yes, Sergeant Greaves. He and those two clowns Bierson and Harley had tromped all over the place, and then Big Sam and his flunkies came along—and don't forget the van, the mobile crime lab. I think they even backed it up over the lawn to the front door in order to load or unload something."

Morris groaned. "That would be their scene-of-crime analysand. It's supposed to scan the whole area with lasers or something and then feed everything it finds into a computer. I heard that what it told them after they had figured out the printouts was that there were two or three fairly large rooms with some furniture in them."

"Jesus!" said Henry.

"Anyway," said Morris, "I don't care whether I could have learned anything from an examination of the ground. What bothers me is that I didn't even consider it."

"Oh, come now, Lieutenant, we can't all be perfect," said Henry, and then added quickly, in order to forestall any platitudes that he was sure Morris had on hand for any such opening, "I'm sure you concentrated your investigation on the inside of the house because you were already certain who you were after, am I right?"

Lieutenant Morris smiled to himself, complacently, Henry thought.

"Tell me, Lieutenant," coaxed Henry, "you knew who had done it all along, didn't you? What was the first clue? When did you first suspect that the—God, I just can't think of Jeanette as an assassin. But when did you first realize that it was she?"

"Well, actually, you know," said Morris, unhesitatingly, if, indeed, his manner of speech could be said to be without hesitation, "when I first came on the scene I had no idea who was involved, so you might say that the first thing that set the course of the investigation was the body itself." Morris had settled back in his chair, and Henry was astute enough to realize that he was in for a treat. This cop was going to unburden himself, although for what reason Henry could not imagine.

"The first thing that caught my attention," continued Morris, "was the wound itself. You may recall—or maybe you don't, considering the state you were in—that there was clotted blood surrounding the opening of the wound and also on the pajamas and robe of the victim. Now, even before the medical examiner's corroboration, one could guess that the victim had been shot, had lain quietly for a while, allowing the blood from the wound to clot and dry, and then had suddenly exerted himself, causing a fresh flow of blood from the wound."

Of course! thought Henry, *The Three Caskets* by John Dickson Carr, the textbook puzzler familiar to everyone who had ever tried to write a locked-room mystery.

"So you might say," continued Morris, "that my initial impression, which determined my whole approach to the case, was that here was a man who was shot some time ago, maybe three or four hours previously, who had suddenly revived and somehow gotten himself drowned in his own swimming pool. I must admit that this first impression dominated all my thinking in regard to this case, even though I knew better and should not have let one theory take over in my conducting of the investigation."

Henry thought he detected a literary note creeping into Morris's discourse, and he was beginning to feel a bit uneasy. What was all this about "initial impression," "theory," and "conducting of the case"? He would have felt much easier if Morris had said something like "I seen it that way and this is what I done," which certainly would have been more in keeping with local constabulary speech patterns. *Now* what was he up to?

"So how did that lead you to your conclusion?"

"Well, for one thing, it ruled you out as a suspect—at least, in my eyes it did. I could hardly believe that you could have shot your neighbor in his own house and then, after the passage of three or four hours, being confronted with his body in his swimming pool, have promptly pulled him out of the water and dutifully called the police. You would more than likely have taken off for parts unknown."

"I certainly would have," agreed Henry. "I was unnerved enough as it was, and I *knew* I hadn't shot Casewait."

"And for another, it kept me from jumping to the obvious conclusion: that the person or persons you heard getting into a car and leaving the scene in a hurry was the killer. No, there had to be someone in the house sometime earlier in the evening—morning, actually—who had shot Casewait, and then there had to be another person in the house who left just as you came out of your house.

"I knew it wasn't a case of forced entry—all the physical evidence ruled that out—and I couldn't believe that it was a mob killing, so it was merely a matter of finding out who had access to the house and whether they could have been here at the time of the murder. As it turned out, everybody within Casewait's immediate circle of family and friends—including you and your wife—could have been."

"But didn't the distances involved throw you off?" asked Henry. "I mean, how could you have suspected someone who was in Paris or Los Angeles of being here in the middle of the night?"

"Well, it was practically forced on me. Think of it; when I first meet the most important person in a murder case, the victim's wife, she has arrived just a short time before after flying in from Los Angeles and driving here from the airport, all done with a minimum of fuss and bother. And while I am here, she receives an overseas call from her stepdaughter, who has just flown into Charles de Gaulle Airport from Lyon after a stopover in Dijon. There was talk of Concordes and jet lag and concern over little annoyances such as getting to and from the airport. If they weren't exactly jet-setters, they were still remarkably comfortable with long-distance travel."

Morris paused for a moment. "Actually," he said, rather reluctantly, Henry thought, "it was Chief Desplaines who pointed out something here that actually set me on the right track."

"Desplaines!" said Henry. "But he hadn't even been to

the scene of the crime or met any of the people involved. How could he have known anything? I thought he was off on another of his jaunts."

"Well, he was, but he does read our reports when he gets back. And these jaunts, as you call them, sometimes yield some valuable results. You've got to remember," said Morris, suddenly coming to the defense of his boss, "that Chief Desplaines is an active and important member of both the International Association of Chiefs of Police *and* the International Federation of Senior Police Officers, and he's one of the few members of either organization who attends all of their conventions and convocations and committee meetings or study groups and whatever else they can think of to take them to exotic places where they can dress up every night and drink as much as they want."

"I see," said Henry, properly chastened.

"Anyway, if there's one thing that the chief knows, it's the world's airports, and he smelled something fishy right away about Miss Casewait's alibi."

"And what was that?" asked Henry.

"Several things. First, what was she doing at Charles de Gaulle, which is a big new plant geared to international travel? The Concorde and seven forty-sevens are the big trade there. A small in-country flight from Lyon would probably land at Le Bourget or Orly. And he also didn't buy that story of hers about her flight being sidetracked to Dijon to convenience some fat-cat businessman. We may think the French are erratic, but I can assure you that they are not in the habit of altering flight plans without extraordinary reasons."

"And from this you deduced that she had spent the night of the murder here instead of in her hotel in Paris?"

"No, but it gave me something to think about. There was the possibility that she could have flown here and back within the course of one day. I believe rock stars do it as a matter of course. I thought I could find out easily by checking her passport, which turned out to be a temporary blind alley."

"Uh, yes," said Henry. "I probably could have helped you out there. I knew from my daughter that Jane had lost her passport—or at least *thought* she had lost it, and had applied for a new one. So she wound up with two perfectly valid passports."

"Yes," said Morris, "and she showed me the one that didn't bear her reentry stamp into France. Well, it was only a chance that she might have overlooked something as obvious as a stamped passport."

"You mean, then, that you actually *did* suspect Jane? I thought I was the only one."

"Oh, definitely. She certainly was acting peculiar—still is, if you ask me. You know, I believe that she *knew* her stepmother had shot Casewait. She could have lain awake that night and listened to them argue, as I'm sure she had done countless times as a young girl. Or she may have awakened and seen her stepmother leave the house. Anyway, I'm pretty sure that she has been covering for her.

"I can't say I blame her, though. Actually, she was the only person who had a strong motive for killing her father. She must have harbored murderous thoughts over the years and probably felt protective of the person who had actually done what she may only have thought of."

"What *did* you consider her motive?" asked Henry. "I agree with you so far, but I'm curious to know what your idea of her grievances were."

"Well, the obvious one is her deformity. I understand that Casewait was somehow the cause of that, smuggling in the pills and practically forcing his wife to take them. Of course, what her feelings are is only conjecture. No one can know how deeply a person can feel about such a thing as a deformity, and how much they blame or don't blame their parents for it. Then there's also the business of her mother's death. *I'm* satisfied it was a suicide, but it can't be proved, of course. However, I'm sure that Miss Casewait was aware of the suspicious nature of that accident, and if she deduced that her mother had been driven to take her own life, then it was one more thing she had against her father.

"And there was the fact, which we just found out, that her father intended to use her for laundering the money he'd held back from Zawwada's employers."

"So you think that he was definitely getting ready to leave the country?"

"I don't think he had any choice. Those people will forgive just about anything except disloyalty, and keeping their money for yourself instead of turning it over to them is about as disloyal as you can get, from their way of looking at it. His daughter's being in Switzerland must have seemed to him a golden opportunity to get the money out of the country and to provide him with a first base abroad. He was pretty knowledgeable about such things, wasn't he? I mean, setting himself up abroad."

"He traveled to Europe quite often, I know that. And he made a few commercials in France and Italy a few years ago, so he must have had to manage some fairly large amounts of money in foreign currency—bank drafts and letters of credit, that sort of thing."

"I can't help wondering if he had any more of those attaché cases stashed away," said Morris. "You might keep your eye open for any more mysterious keys. What's the matter, Mr. Wilnot? You look skeptical. You find it hard to believe Casewait's operation could have been larger than we've been able to determine?"

"No, it's not about that," said Henry, "I'm prepared to believe anything about Casewait. What I find difficult to believe is that all of your suspicions about Jane were founded on your uncertainty over the airport she says she landed at."

"It was pretty vague, I must admit, but it was more than a hunch or any intuition on my part. For instance, when you called Miss Casewait's hotel in Paris, you didn't actually talk to the manager or the desk clerk there, did you?"

"No, I left that to my wife."

"So we had two people talking together who had English as a second language. I don't mean to imply that your wife's English is inadequate, but just what did she say when she relayed the message to you?"

"As far as I can remember, she said that the hotel was holding Jane's room for her. She hadn't arrived yet, because she was held up in Dijon—at least, that's what she told us later."

"Ah, see, now that's what I had trouble with," said Morris. "I believed, as you all did, that Miss Casewait had arrived at the hotel the morning *before* Casewait had been shot, received his message to call her, and then departed for the airport. The hotel had agreed to hold her room until she *returned* from the U.S., but we all believed that the hotel was holding her room until she *arrived* from Dijon. It was only when I realized that your wife may have misunderstood or hadn't asked for clarification of the hotel clerk's information that I decided to check further. A telex to Paris cleared the whole thing up."

"But after all that, what made you decide that Jeanette instead of Jane had shot Casewait?"

"It was that hotel again," said Morris. "How did you find out its name, for instance?"

"Jeanette told us. She said she'd had a letter from Jane, one of those blue aerograms that are so hard to open without destroying the message."

"Did you actually read it?"

"No, she was waving it around, as I recall, but I never actually saw it."

"She didn't give it to you to copy down the address or telephone number?"

"No. As a matter of fact, she wrote down the number for me, which seemed unnecessary to me at the time."

"So there you are," said Morris. "From the very beginning, everybody in this case has denied any communication with anybody else prior to the shooting. Miss Casewait, even after confessing that she had been in contact with her father, denied talking or writing to anyone else."

"So how did Jeanette get that aerogram, and how did she know Jane's address in Paris?"

"That's what I asked myself," said Morris. "And I had to conclude that she had gotten it from Casewait himself, here in this house on the night he was shot. And she told us as much just a few minutes ago."

"I get it," said Henry, rather disappointed. "And that's all?"

"I'm afraid so," said Morris. He paused, then said, "You know, Mr. Wilnot, it might interest you to learn that you were my strongest suspect, particularly at the end."

Henry was startled. "But how could I be?" he protested. "You've said two or three times that you knew I hadn't shot Casewait."

"Yes," said Morris, "I knew that you hadn't *shot* him, but I wasn't so sure that you hadn't killed him. You see, Mr. Wilnot, the medical examiner and I, and of course Chief Desplaines, are the only people who knew that Casewait actually died by drowning, and today was the first time I revealed it to anyone else."

"I don't understand," said Henry. "When did I ever say that he had drowned?"

"When we first met. I have it here in my notebook. You said, 'All I know is that he got himself shot and then drowned in his wretched pool.' " He smiled to himself as he repocketed his notebook. "You certainly had it in for that pool."

"You have no idea . . . " said Henry. "But that seems a rather flimsy excuse for suspecting someone of murder. I mean, anyone pulling a dead man out of the water would assume that he had drowned, even if he did have a bullet hole in his chest. And for another thing, how could I have done it without getting all wet? Wouldn't there have been a bit of a struggle? After all, Casewait had managed to make it to the pool in the first place and probably had some strength left in him even after he fell into the water."

"Ah, but Mr. Wilnot, your ensemble was a study in drip-dry, and anyway, there was that handy pool skimmer. It could have been used to hold his head underwater."

"Lieutenant," said Henry, "are you seriously accusing me of—"

"No, no," interrupted Morris, halting Henry in mid dudgeon. "Nothing of the sort. I was just trying to show you the number of possibilities that are presented in the investigation of a murder. Or more properly, in this case, a simple shooting."

"But why are you telling me all this, Lieutenant, unless it's to provoke me? In fact, it seems to me that you've taken me into your confidence much more than one would expect from a detective investigating a homicide."

Morris appeared to be embarrassed. He said, tentatively, "Well, there *is* something I would like to take up with you, Mr. Wilnot. You see, I have been on this job for nearly twenty years, and given the nature of the area, the social mix, you might say, I have investigated some very, uh, interesting cases, many of which were never pursued to their limits, what with charges being dropped, decisions being made on a higher level—well, you see what I mean, Mr. Wilnot."

Henry did indeed see what he meant, and his heart sank into his chukka boot. "You feel that you have a book in you, don't you, Lieutenant?" he said.

"Well, yes, I rather think I do. But since the material is sensitive, it can't just be a recounting of my cases. It would have to be fiction. A novel." And having said that, Lieutenant Morris hung his head in shame and remorse.

"I don't see anything wrong with that," said Henry. "God knows there's been enough of that sort of thing, what with that fellow out on the Coast—what's his name?"

"Wambaugh!" Morris said, spitting out the word bitterly.

"But I don't understand your problem," said Henry. "You shouldn't have any trouble assembling the material. I've heard that you fellows are great on paperwork—by necessity, by necessity!" he added quickly when Morris raised his head and glared at him. "Also, I believe that the police academy now has an excellent course in creative writing."

"Yes, but that was after my time," said Morris. "We older officers just weren't properly trained." In his agitation, Morris rose from his chair and began striding about the room. He finally paused in front of Henry and said, "Do you know that my stuff has been turned down by *Investigating Officer*?"

To Henry, who thought that he himself had been rejected by every magazine in existence, this came as a revelation. "Do you mean there's a magazine called *Investigating Officer* that publishes fiction?"

"Well, not exactly fiction, but impressions, musings, mood pieces on crime and violence; that sort of thing," said Morris.

"I shouldn't think you would have any trouble with that," said Henry. "You're obviously literate and well spoken, and I'm sure your experiences are interesting."

"That's just it," said Morris. "I don't have any trouble telling my stories to someone else, or writing up reports on my cases, but when it comes to having people act by themselves and then talk in a voice different from my own, I can't seem to do anything. Like when one person says something and another answers him right back."

"You mean you aren't very good at dialogue."

"Exactly," said Morris with some relief.

Henry thought long and hard before he next spoke. "Lieutenant," he said, "perhaps I could be of some assistance to you. If you would like me to look at your manuscript, I would be glad to give you some advice." And, he might have added, introduce you to my agent, arrange meetings with some editors who owe me, and grease the skids along the dismal way to publication, which can only end with heartache, disillusion, and a handful of grudges that will last you for the rest of your life.

"Why, that's very kind of you," said Morris, brightening. "As a matter of fact I do have a few things I could show you." To Henry's relief, he did not whip out a sheaf of foolscap, or worse yet, a computer printout. "I'll send them over tomorrow. Harley or Bierson can drop them off while on patrol. You know them, don't you, Harley and Bierson?"

"Oh, yes, I know them quite well," said Henry, rising slowly from his chair as though emerging from a Henry James story about art and artists. "I will look forward to receiving them."

Epilogue

HENRY WILNOT STEPPED out onto his back porch and greeted the waning summer's day with a contented countenance, the first time he had been able to do so in quite a while. His feeling of well-being was occasioned by his having divested himself shortly before of any responsibility for the estate of his recently deceased neighbor, Joseph Casewait.

Henry was now mercifully alone. He had convinced Erica, his wife, to proceed with her trip to Germany to visit her mother and their daughter, who had definitely taken up residence in Stuttgart. Before she left, Erica had made a full confession to him of her affair with Casewait. It had proved to be a dismal business, with Casewait playing footsie with her for several years before finally luring her to his loathsome pool for skinny-dipping while Henry had been away on one of his rare business trips for a magazine he guest-edited occasionally. She couldn't explain what had led her to give in to Casewait, except that she felt that his attentions were somehow proof of her femininity and attractiveness. It was all very well that Henry loved her and provided for her, but then, let's face it, Henry would have probably done that for any woman he happened to marry. Whereas Casewait chased after anything in skirts—an old-fashioned phrase if ever there was one, thought Henry—and to miss out on his attentions was somehow to be, well, *slighted*, in a sense. It seemed to Henry that there were far too many *somehows* in this explanation, but he bought it anyway, probably because he was disposed to buy it. He could not help reminding Erica, however, that he had never been unfaithful to her, which was perhaps a cheap shot, but it would prepare the ground for any unlikely peccadilloes he might have in mind for the future. The thought of a certain Miss Nathan somehow lingered on the edge of his consciousness.

Jeanette was back in California, to which she had gratefully fled after the court had laid on her a number of restrictions that Henry doubted could ever be fully monitored on either coast. And Jane was in Paris, where she had decided to stay after her maharishis had taken their traveling road show to yet another of the world's capitals. She would return to her native shores when probate of her father's will was completed and she could come into her inheritance, which was now in the hands of the capable Miss Nathan. Henry had relinquished his duties as coexecutor of Casewait's estate on the grounds of imminent pauperdom if he did not attend to his own affairs first.

A car had drawn up at the entrance to Henry's driveway and two men were getting out. One was tall and possessed of a slender elegance, enhanced by his clothes, which consisted of blue blazer, beige trousers, button-down blue shirt open at the collar, and polished loafers. A walking cliché, thought Henry, but one found largely in the better schools, the better jobs, the better restaurants, and the better parts of town.

The other man was short and stockily built, although with an overall roundness to him. He wore faded blue jeans and an untucked white oxford shirt, the tails of which were knotted in front, exposing a bare midriff. He had on wooden-soled sandals attached by leather thongs to the dirtiest pair of feet north of the state of Chihuahua.

The tall man was blond with carefully trimmed longish hair; the other one had sparse light brown hair that clung to his head in ringlets. As they walked up the driveway, the short one said, "My *gawd*, did you ever *see* anything so country-cottagey?" and the other replied between clenched teeth, "*Shut* up!"

Henry descended the porch steps to meet them. "Can I help you?" he asked genially.

"Why, yes," said the tall one, smiling. "You're Mr. Wilnot, aren't you?"

"Yes."

"Well, uh, my name is Birmingham. Thomas Birmingham. And this is Benjy." He nodded toward his companion. "Didn't Miss Nathan call about us?"

"Miss Nathan? No, I haven't heard from her. Not today, anyway."

"Hmm," said Birmingham. "Well, you see, we'll be moving in next door, so I thought we'd drop by to say—"

"But," said Henry, "I thought you were mar—"

Benjy, smirking and making a mocking little bow, sang in a prissy voice, "Won't—you be—my neighbor?"

If you have enjoyed this book and would like to receive details of other Walker mystery titles, please write to:

Mystery Editor
Walker and Company
720 Fifth Avenue
New York, NY 10019